A Winning Entry

"Dylan, I found your entry for the big state essay contest," Elizabeth said. "You've got to get it in the mail tonight or it will be disqualified!"

There was a long silence at the other end of the line, then Dylan said, "It doesn't matter. Throw it away."

The line went dead. Elizabeth stared at the receiver in her hand, shocked. Throw away this great essay? He must be kidding.

Elizabeth replaced the receiver slowly, then went back to her room. She sat down on her bed, still holding Dylan's paper. What should she do? She couldn't throw away an essay as good as this one.

She sat in silence for several minutes, worrying over the problem, and then a startling solution came to her. . . .

Bantam Skylark Books in the SWEET VALLEY TWINS series
Ask your bookseller for the books you have missed

SWEET VALLEY TWINS

Second Best

Written by
Jamie Suzanne

Created by
FRANCINE PASCAL

A BANTAM SKYLARK BOOK®
TORONTO • NEW YORK • LONDON • SYDNEY • AUCKLAND

RL 4, 008–012

SECOND BEST
A Bantam Skylark Book / February 1988

Bantam Books are published by Bantam Books, a division of Bantam
Doubleday Dell Publishing Group, Inc. Its trademark, consisting of the
words "Bantam Books" and the portrayal of a rooster, is Registered in
U.S. Patent and Trademark Office and in other countries. Marca Regis-
trada. Bantam Books, 666 Fifth Avenue, New York, New York 10103.

PRINTED IN THE UNITED STATES OF AMERICA

O   0 9 8 7 6 5 4 3 2 1

Second Best

One

◇

"Guess what, Mom!" Elizabeth and Jessica Wakefield exclaimed in unison as they burst through the door into the sunny, tiled kitchen of their Spanish-style home. The two girls glanced at each other and giggled.

Alice Wakefield, their mother, smiled at her 12-year-old twin daughters. Looking at them was almost like seeing double. Both girls had the same sun-streaked blond hair, the same blue-green eyes, and even the same dimple in their left cheeks. But Jessica's hair fell in soft waves around her oval face, while Elizabeth pulled her hair back to the sides, pinning it with gold barrettes. And although they looked so much alike, they were very different.

"There's a statewide essay contest—" Elizabeth started.

"Kimberly Haver's planning this incredible birthday party—" Jessica interrupted.

"The topic is freedom of speech, and the winner gets a gold medal—"

"Everybody at Sweet Valley Middle School is going. It's the biggest party of the whole year—"

"Not to mention a hundred-dollar prize!" Elizabeth continued.

"And I absolutely *have* to go. I mean, Kimberly would really be disappointed if I couldn't!" Jessica concluded, watching her mother anxiously.

"Sounds like you girls had an exciting day at school," Mrs. Wakefield said. "Now why don't you tell me your news one at a time."

Before either of the girls could say another word, Steven Wakefield, the twins' fourteen-year-old brother, spoke up.

"Big deal," he scoffed, dipping one finger into a bowl of fudge icing Mrs. Wakefield had just finished making. "If you want to hear some real news, let me tell you about the plans for our sports banquet—"

"Steven . . ." Jessica rolled her eyes. "All you ever talk about is basketball. Isn't that true, Lizzie?" She turned to her sister for reinforcement.

Elizabeth nodded. "Especially since the junior varsity team won the league championship," she pointed out. Although only a freshman at Sweet Valley High, Steven was one of the star players on the J.V. team.

"My game's more interesting than somebody's

dumb birthday party," Steven argued. Tall and dark haired, he bore a strong resemblance to their father, while the two girls had inherited their mother's looks. Steven licked the chocolate off his finger and reached for the bowl of icing once again, but Mrs. Wakefield moved it out of reach before he could get his hands on it.

"No more tasting before dinner," she said firmly. "Girls, set the table. We'll talk about the contest, and the party, at dinner."

The two girls hurried upstairs. Elizabeth paused in her neat blue-and-cream-colored bedroom just long enough to drop her books on the bed. Then she went into the bathroom that connected her room to her sister's to wash her hands and comb her hair.

"Better hurry, Jess," she called. "Mom's waiting for us." When Jessica didn't answer, Elizabeth glanced through the open door. Jessica's bed was buried beneath a mound of clothes.

Until the beginning of this school year, the sisters had shared a room, and Jessica's mess had always irritated Elizabeth. Moving into separate rooms had been a relief, though Elizabeth sometimes missed Jessica's company. Just this year, too, the twins had dropped their old habit of dressing alike and had begun to develop different interests and acquire different sets of friends. Elizabeth had taken up writing for the sixth-grade paper, while Jessica spent her time making up new cheers with the Boosters cheering squad, made up mostly of Unicorns. She also liked to gossip with her friends from the Unicorn Club. But, despite their differences, they were still the best of friends.

At this moment, Jessica Wakefield was sitting on the floor beside her bed with her head in her hands.

"What's the matter?" Elizabeth asked.

"Oh, Lizzie," Jessica wailed. "If Mom and Dad don't let me go to Kimberly's party, I'll just die! I've already been grounded for over a week!"

Elizabeth was torn between sympathy for Jessica and memories of the giant pack of lies that had gotten Jessica into trouble in the first place.

"Oh, Jess. You should never have lied to them about dating that high school boy," she pointed out.

Jessica made a face. "Please, Lizzie, no lectures," she begged. "I said I'd never do it again!"

Elizabeth sighed. "I'll cross my fingers for you," she said. She gave her sister a quick hug, then they both hurried down the stairs.

As the twins set the table, Mrs. Wakefield inspected a steaming dish of baked chicken that was in the oven.

"Here's Daddy," Elizabeth said when she heard the front door open.

"Oh, gosh," Jessica murmured. "I didn't think Dad was coming home for dinner tonight."

Elizabeth glanced at her sister. "Don't give up yet," she whispered. "Wait and see what Mom and Dad say."

Both the twins sat down to dinner feeling tense.

Elizabeth's own conscience was clear, but she couldn't help worrying about what would happen to Jessica. Kimberly's party would definitely be more fun if Jessica were there—that was, if they were even invited.

As for Jessica, toying with the chicken and rice on her plate, her fear continued to grow as she waited for her parents to discuss her fate.

As soon as Mr. and Mrs. Wakefield had listened to Steven's enthusiastic account of the upcoming sports banquet, Elizabeth had her turn to explain about the state essay contest.

"A lot of the kids at school are going to enter. Mr. Bowman, our English teacher, said he'd give us extra credit for writing the essays, too," Elizabeth told them. Mr. Bowman was not only Elizabeth's favorite faculty member but also advisor to the *Sweet Valley Sixers*, the sixth-grade student newspaper.

"That sounds very exciting," Mr. Wakefield said.

"Not as exciting as Kimberly's party!" Jessica exclaimed, unable to contain herself any longer. "She's inviting the whole seventh grade, plus a few of the sixth graders—the ones who are really mature—"

"That leaves you out," Steven said with a grin.

Jessica's quick temper flared. "It does not! Of course she'll ask me, and Elizabeth, too," she added as an afterthought. "And her parents are renting strobe lights, and a *huge* sound system."

"How juvenile." Steven snorted.

Mrs. Wakefield frowned at her son. With a significant glance toward her husband, she said, "We received something interesting in the mail today."

Both girls looked at their mother in anticipation.

"The Sweet Valley Middle School report cards have arrived."

Elizabeth relaxed, knowing that her grades were always good, but Jessica fidgeted and looked at her plate.

"And?" Jessica held her breath. She knew perfectly well that if she paid more attention to her schoolwork she could do as well as her sister. But how could she be expected to devote all her time to studying when there were so many more interesting things happening at school?

"Jessica," Mr. Wakefield began, sharing a sober look with his wife. "I have to tell you I was very surprised when your mother called me today to tell me about your report card. I thought you had promised to spend more time on your schoolwork."

"I did. I—have," Jessica sputtered.

"Then why haven't your grades improved?" her father asked.

Jessica, aware that everyone at the table was looking at her, searched for an appropriate answer.

"Well, there was the Mini-Olympics. I spent a lot of time working on that. I *was* chairman, after all, and you all agreed it was a very worthwhile project."

"That was weeks ago," Steven pointed out. Jessica frowned at him, then glanced toward her father for some sign of understanding, but his expression didn't soften.

"And what about my sprained ankle? It's hard to study when your ankle hurts!"

Steven pretended to wipe away a tear. Jessica forgot she was trying to look pathetic and glared at him.

But Mr. Wakefield wasn't amused. "I'm afraid that isn't good enough, Jessica. Your mother and I were discussing this morning whether you'd been grounded long enough. But now, after receiving this report card, I'm afraid we're going to have to continue your restrictions for at least another two weeks until we see some improvement at school."

"Two weeks? That's inhuman!" Jessica blurted out. "You can't!"

Mrs. Wakefield's blue-green eyes softened just a tiny bit in response to her daughter's distress. Jessica glanced at her mother, hoping for a last-minute reprieve. But Mrs. Wakefield shook her head.

"I'm sorry, Jessica. But we did warn you."

Elizabeth bit her lip in sympathy, while Steven grinned openly. But Jessica was too upset to notice either of them.

Two weeks! That would mean that she couldn't go to Kimberly's birthday party! She had to think of something fast to get out of this mess.

"I'll bring up my grades," Jessica promised quickly. "I'll—I'll study every night—"

She could see no sign of yielding in either of her

parents' faces. Jessica glanced at her sister and suddenly remembered Elizabeth's comment.
"The school project—if I work extra hard and make a really good grade, that'll bring up my average."

Jessica thought that her mother was considering the idea, but Mr. Wakefield still looked unconvinced.

"I'm not sure that one project will make that much difference," he pointed out.

But Elizabeth, anxious to come to her twin's aid, interrupted. "This project is really important, Dad," she assured him. "It'll make up a big part of our grade, because we're spending so much time on it. The teachers are even combining the sixth and seventh grades to make up the groups."

Mr. Wakefield raised his brows. "If it's a major grade, maybe . . ." he began.

With new hope, Jessica pressed her advantage. "Just give me a two-week trial, and if you don't see a real improvement, *then* you can ground me again," she suggested, her tone noble. *And I'll be able to go to Kimberly's big party, either way,* she thought.

"All right," her dad agreed. "Two weeks."

"You won't be sorry," Jessica promised.

Mrs. Wakefield stood up from the table. "I'll get dessert," she said.

Steven, who looked disappointed that Jessica had gotten off so easily, perked up at the mention of dessert.

"I want a big piece of cake," he said, hurrying into the kitchen behind his mother.

Elizabeth leaned over to touch her twin's shoulder. "I'll help you with your project, Jess," she offered.

"Oh, thanks, Lizzie. But I may not need you. I'll probably have the Unicorns in my group, and I just know we'll come up with something terrific."

Elizabeth looked doubtful. The members of the Unicorn Club were Jessica's favorite friends at Sweet Valley Middle School. They were an exclusive group of pretty and popular girls who considered themselves, like the mythical animal for which their club was named, very special. Elizabeth wasn't much interested in the club. She found their gossip about boys and clothes rather dull, and she knew for sure they weren't the best scholars at school. "Are you sure?" Elizabeth asked. "The teachers will be assigning the groups, you know, and anyhow—"

"I'll manage it," Jessica assured her sister airily. "And we'll ask for Bruce Patman and Jerry McAllister and maybe that new McKay boy—the one who's so cute."

Elizabeth drew her brows together as she tried to remember. "Dylan?" she asked.

"Who?" Jessica looked blank. "Oh, him—of course not. He's not cute at all! And he's totally boring, besides. I mean his brother, Tom."

Elizabeth wasn't at all sure that this list of names was going to ensure a good grade for her sister. "I hope you're right, Jess. Mom and Dad are really serious about this, you know."

"Your sister's right, Jessica," Mr. Wakefield added. "You're going to have to really put a lot of effort into this project."

"I will, Dad," Jessica promised. "It might even turn out to be fun!"

"I hope you know what you're doing," Elizabeth murmured under her breath. Leave it to Jessica to turn an important school project into another exciting social event.

Two

◇

On Tuesday morning Elizabeth sat at the breakfast table enjoying the last mouthful of her waffle.

"Where on earth is Jessica?" Mrs. Wakefield asked, worried. "At this rate, she's not going to have time to eat her breakfast."

Elizabeth shrugged. "She was in the bathroom when I came downstairs," she told her mother.

Mrs. Wakefield looked at her watch. "I'm going into town for an appointment with a client this morning. I think I'd better drop you two off at school. You're not going to have time to walk at this rate." Mrs. Wakefield, an interior designer, worked part-time for a local firm.

Elizabeth nodded, licking a drop of maple syrup off her fork. "I'll tell her to hurry," she offered, getting up and running toward the stairs. She discovered Jessica hidden in the recesses of her cluttered closet.

"We're going to be late to school, Jess," Elizabeth said. "Mom wants us to hurry up."

"I'll be there in a minute," Jessica called from the back of the closet. She emerged a moment later with an armload of clothes, added them to the existing pile on her bed, and began to look through them critically.

"What are you doing?" Elizabeth asked curiously. "I thought that pink skirt was too small for you. And you said you hated that green sweater Aunt Mary sent you for Christmas."

"I do," Jessica assured her sister, sounding very pleased with herself. "But I have this great idea!"

"If you don't hurry, you're going to get into more trouble," Elizabeth warned.

"Don't be a pain, Lizzie," Jessica complained. But she left the pile of clothes on her bed, grabbed her school books, and ran for the stairs.

On the way to Sweet Valley Middle School, Jessica got permission from her mother to donate some of her outgrown clothing to the school project.

"I usually give those things to the thrift shop," Mrs. Wakefield said, "but if it will help your project, of course you may use them, Jess. I'm pleased to see you so enthusiastic about this special project."

Jessica looked smug. Elizabeth couldn't help feeling a tiny twinge of suspicion, but she waited until they got out of the car and waved good-bye to their mother before she added, "That green sweater isn't too small on you."

"So I'll sneak in a few extra things that I'd like to get rid of. That will give me a good excuse to go shopping," Jessica explained, completely untroubled by this slight deception.

Elizabeth sighed. "Just how is this going to help your grade, anyhow? I haven't heard about a special school project involving old clothes."

"You'll see," Jessica promised. "Lila, Ellen, hi. Over here," she called.

Elizabeth hesitated as Jessica's two best friends, members of the Unicorn Club, approached. Normally she would have left at this point, but this morning she lingered, curious to hear more about Jessica's idea.

"Hi, Jessica," Ellen Riteman said. "Wait till you see the new outfit Lila bought for Kimberly's birthday party! It's gorgeous and makes Lila look like she should be in high school, at least!"

"Are you getting something new for the party, Jessica?" Lila asked.

Everyone knew that Lila Fowler's father was on his way to being one of the richest men in Sweet Valley. He spoiled his daughter terribly to make up for the lack of time he spent with her. It seemed as though Lila had something new to wear to school every single day. *Some things are just not fair,* Jessica thought, a frown momentarily darkening her face. But Lila was her best friend, even if she was sometimes envious of her.

"I haven't asked my mother yet," Jessica said. "I had something else on my mind. I was thinking we should have a Unicorn meeting today, because I want to talk about that special project we have to do."

Both girls stared at Jessica in surprise. Talking about schoolwork instead of new clothes definitely did not sound like Jessica.

"Who wants to talk about *that*?" Lila objected, wrinkling her nose.

Jessica considered admitting that she had to get a good grade to bring up her average at school or face being grounded by her parents, but quickly decided against it. *Lila* never got grounded. Instead Jessica began to talk quickly.

"No, listen, it's going to be really fun. You know how we have to form our own company, and create a product or perform a service, and write reports and keep books and do all that stuff to show how a modern business works? Well, I had this great idea—we can start our own boutique!"

Ellen's eyes widened, and even Lila looked impressed.

"Jessica, you really have been thinking about this, haven't you?" Elizabeth said. "That is a great idea!"

"It'll really impress the teachers, and think of the fun we can have. We'll set up a booth, decorate it, sell the clothes to the other kids. We'll be the hit of the school! I can't wait." Jessica could barely contain her excitement.

"Where are we going to get the clothes?" Ellen asked.

"That's simple. Just go through our closets and pull out all the stuff that's too small, or out of style. Not everyone is as fashionably dressed as the Unicorns. The other kids will love our old clothes!"

Elizabeth frowned at the unconscious insult in her twin's statement, but the two other girls saw nothing wrong with what she had said.

"I think you're right, Jessica. It sounds like it could be fun. I was *dreading* having to do this special assignment," Lila said.

Jessica glowed. "And we'll have all the Unicorns in our group," she told the girls.

"Jessica," Elizabeth interrupted. "You know there's no guarantee you'll all end up together."

"So we'll make a special request," Jessica said with a shrug. "And we'll ask for some of the cutest boys. Bruce Patman, and maybe that new McKay boy. . . ."

"Tom?" Lila pursed her lips, then nodded in agreement. "He was just elected president of the tennis club; he deserves to work with the Unicorns. But not his nerdy brother."

"Of course not. Who wants him?" Jessica agreed. "And you can be in our group too, Lizzie," she offered, suddenly remembering her sister.

"Thanks, Jess." Elizabeth shook her head at Jessica's ability to ignore the facts. "But I think we'll have to wait and see which group we end up in, and besides, I have an idea of my own."

The sound of the first bell made them all jump. "I've got to go. See you later, Jessica," Elizabeth said, running off toward her first class.

Jessica, already absorbed in planning the Unicorn boutique with her friends, didn't even hear.

Three

◇

The morning went by quickly, and Elizabeth never had a chance to find her own friends to tell them *her* idea for the class project. So when it was time for lunch period, she hurried to the cafeteria to catch up with Amy Sutton and Julie Porter, two of her closest friends. Halfway down the hall, she realized that she'd left her notebook in class. Turning, she ran back toward the classroom. She could see two boys standing at the back of the room. She could tell that they were arguing.

"I don't want to!" one boy said.

"Come on," the other urged. "Why won't you come to the meeting after school?"

Elizabeth recognized one of the boys as Tom McKay. Although relatively new to the school, he was already well known. All the sixth-grade girls agreed he was very, very cute. He was a talented athlete, a good student, and had a great sense of humor.

When the other boy turned slightly, Elizabeth could see it was Dylan McKay, Tom's older brother. Dylan, a skinny seventh grader, looked awkward and ill at ease beside his athletically built younger brother.

"Would you quit telling me what to do!"

Tom flushed slightly. "I just wanted—"

"Who cares what you want?" Dylan interrupted, his tone gruff. "I'm older than you are. Why should *you* tell *me* what to do?"

"I'm not telling you what to do," Tom retorted. "I just thought maybe you'd want to get involved. . . ."

"That meeting's for the student government. You belong there, you're one of the room representatives. I wasn't even *nominated* for room representative—much less elected. I'm not interested in student government, okay? Why don't you just leave me alone?"

"Anyone can come and work on the posters," Tom continued, frowning. "Maybe you could meet some more people, Dylan. Make some friends."

"I don't care about making friends," Dylan muttered, kicking the closest desk with his sneaker. "*You're* the smart, popular one. And every family has to have a dummy, too. Why should ours be any different?"

Tom looked uncomfortable. "Don't put yourself down," he told his brother.

In the doorway, Elizabeth felt her conscience stirring. She didn't mean to eavesdrop, but she had to get her notebook before the next class. While she tried to decide what to do, she saw Tom move toward the front of the room.

"I'm going to lunch. Want to eat with me?" Tom seemed to offer a truce, but his brother wouldn't meet his eyes.

"In a minute. You go ahead."

Elizabeth drew a deep breath and walked into the classroom, trying to look as if she'd just arrived. She met Tom heading toward the door.

"Hi," she said brightly. "I forgot my notebook."

Tom smiled at her. He had an engaging grin that lit up his blue eyes. "Better hurry," he advised. "You wouldn't want to miss any of the great cafeteria food."

"That would be awful," Elizabeth joked back. She found her notebook inside her desk, added it to the books in her arms, and turned to leave.

"Hi, Dylan," Elizabeth said as she passed him on her way out.

The taller boy didn't even answer.

Elizabeth shrugged and hurried off to lunch. No wonder Dylan hadn't made any friends, she thought. He didn't seem to want any!

Dylan McKay, left alone in the empty classroom, stared blindly at the blackboard. Girls, especially pretty girls, always left him tongue-tied. He never knew what to say to them! Elizabeth Wakefield seemed so friendly, but she couldn't really want to talk to him. She was pretty and popular, and probably much more interested in his brother.

Dylan was used to being the boy everyone forgot. In the fifth grade, his class had had spelling bees every Friday, and Dylan was always the last kid to be picked—even though he was a good speller. It made him dread Fridays.

And when the boys played baseball or basketball during gym class, the rest of the guys never wanted Dylan on their team. "You can't even hit the ball," they would scoff. "Your little brother is a better player than you are!"

The awful thing was that their taunt was true. Tom had always been a good athlete. All sports came easily to him.

Now Tom, after only a few months of tennis lessons, could beat half the boys at the middle school. Whatever Tom touched turned to gold.

For his part, Dylan had begun to avoid team sports whenever possible. But even off the field, Dylan couldn't seem to make anything go right. Tom always had a joke or a friendly comment for anyone who passed by him in the hallway. Dylan always wound up walking to class alone.

He shook his head. Now that Tom and Elizabeth were out of sight, he sat down in the empty classroom. He was in no hurry to face the crowded cafeteria. Besides, today Dylan had something else on his mind. He opened his notebook and flipped through several pages filled with his large, slanted scrawl.

He was interested in the statewide essay contest that had recently been announced, although he would never have admitted it. He had always liked to scribble down his private thoughts. He'd never shown his work to anyone because he was always too afraid of being ridiculed. The contest topic, freedom of speech, appealed to Dylan. How awful it would be not to be able to speak or write about whatever you wanted to. He had been so inspired by the topic, he had already written a couple of rough drafts.

He looked over the most recent one. He had put a lot of work into it, and for a moment he thought it might even be good.

But then again, maybe not. When had Dylan McKay ever done anything that was really good?

Elizabeth picked up a tray and made her way through the lunch line. When she reached the long lunch tables, she located Amy Sutton, her best friend, who was faithfully saving her a place. Elizabeth hurried to sit down beside her.

"What took you so long?" Amy asked.

"I forgot my notebook and had to go back to class to get it," Elizabeth explained. "Amy, do you know Dylan McKay?"

"Who?" Amy frowned in concentration. "Don't you mean Tom? Cute, with blond hair. He's in my math class."

"No. I mean Dylan," Elizabeth corrected. "I think he's a seventh grader. He's taller than his brother and has darker hair."

"And isn't half as cute," Amy pointed out bluntly. "Yes, I know who you mean. He's the guy who never talks to anyone. He's a real loner."

"I wonder," Elizabeth murmured. Remembering the scene she had just witnessed, she felt a stirring of sympathy for the tall, awkward boy. Maybe he just felt overshadowed by his popular brother.

But Amy had more important matters to discuss. "What are we going to do for the big project?" Amy asked. "Have you had any good ideas yet for a student company?"

"Well . . ." Elizabeth hesitated, dipping her nacho in the thick cheese sauce and taking a bite. "Jessica wants to manage a boutique."

"Clothes?" Amy looked alarmed. "Is that what you want to do, too? I thought we were going to choose something interesting!"

"We are." Elizabeth said. "I didn't promise I would work with Jessica."

"The teachers are going to assign the groups, anyhow," Amy reminded her.

"I know," Elizabeth said. "But you know Jessica. She thinks she can persuade the teachers to do what she wants."

"Jessica gets her own way entirely too often as it is," Amy grumbled.

Elizabeth grinned, remembering how often Jessica had cajoled her into doing special favors for her. "She can be awfully charming when she wants to be," she admitted. "But then, that's Jessica!"

"I just hope you and I end up in the same group." Amy sighed. She poked a straw into her carton of milk and took a long drink. "Have you finished your essay yet—the one you're entering in the state contest?"

"Almost," Elizabeth answered. "I've worked on it for three days. I should have it ready by tomorrow."

"I bet you have a good chance at winning," Amy said loyally. "You're such a good writer."

"Thanks." Elizabeth smiled. She loved books, and her ambition was to be a writer someday. "I did the best I could, but there will be lots of entries. I've heard some of the others are very good. Mr. Bowman told our class that Tom McKay's essay was excellent."

Amy, absorbed in her friend's comments, didn't notice the tall boy who had paused just behind Elizabeth.

"Sounds like you'll have some tough competition. Maybe Tom McKay will win. He's awfully talented."

Elizabeth didn't see the boy behind her, either, and she and Amy continued to chat until lunch period was over.

Dylan McKay walked slowly past Elizabeth, feeling a hollowness inside his stomach that had nothing to do with hunger. He set his lunch down on an empty table in the back of the cafeteria and found that his appetite had disappeared.

He had worked so hard on his essay and had been planning to show it to his English teacher tomorrow before mailing it in. Now there was no point. Tom already had a winning entry.

Dylan poked at his food, feeling sick inside. What had made him think this contest would be any different? Tom was a winner; Dylan was a loser. That's the way it always was, and that's the way it always would be.

Four

◇

"Oh, please, Mr. Nydick." Jessica smiled sweetly at the social studies teacher the next morning. "If the Unicorns and I could work together in one group, I just know that we could do a super job. And I really want a good grade on this project."

The teacher raised his brows at Jessica's unusual enthusiasm and then smiled back at her. "I'm glad to see that you're really interested, Jessica. But the teachers will assign all the sixth and seventh graders to their groups. I'm afraid you and your friends will have to take your chances."

Jessica's smile faded, and she looked distinctly sulky. She walked toward the bleachers where Lila and the other Unicorns were waiting, along with the rest of the combined sixth and seventh graders. As

Jessica approached, Lila called out to her over the noisy chatter. "What did he say?"

Jessica hesitated before answering. She hated to admit failure, and she'd been boasting earlier that she'd be able to get all the Unicorns together in one group.

"Mr. Nydick said that if we all worked together," she said at last, "we might make the other groups look bad."

"That's true," Lila agreed.

"But he said he'd do what he could," Jessica went on, already half believing her own story. "We'll see."

Jessica sat down beside Lila as the last of the students straggled into the gym. Mr. Bowman walked up to the microphone. Several of the sixth- and seventh-grade teachers stood beside him, each holding a sheet of paper.

"Okay, everybody," Mr. Bowman said. "Settle down."

Gradually the talking subsided, and the restless crowd of middle schoolers shifted their attention to the English teacher.

"Okay," he repeated. "Today we're going to divide into our groups—"

Lila gave Jessica a significant look. Jessica slipped her hands into her jeans pockets and crossed her fingers for luck.

"We've already explained a bit about your assignment," Mr. Bowman went on. "The purpose of this project is to form a company. Once your group is selected, you are to get together and decide what your company will do. You may make a product, sell a service, or do anything that real companies can do."

Jessica wished he would hurry up and start assigning the groups.

"And everyone must have a job; everyone must make a contribution," the English teacher continued. "You may elect a president and vice presidents, managers—whatever you decide you need to run your company. You must name your company, write planning reports, keep records, plan a way to distribute your product, advertise your services—in short, do everything required to run a successful company. I will advise one group, while Mr. Nydick, Mrs. Arnette . . ."

"Oh no. Not the Hairnet," Jessica groaned. The old-fashioned social studies teacher always wore a hairnet to keep any stray hairs from escaping out of the bun on the back of her neck. "I hope we don't get stuck with her."

"—and the rest of the teachers will each advise one of the other groups. Your groups will be made up of equal numbers of sixth and seventh graders."

A few feet from Jessica, Elizabeth sat beside Amy, and the two friends exchanged slightly worried looks.

"I hope we get into the same group," Amy whispered.

"Me, too," Elizabeth agreed. "I asked Mr. Bowman if he would let the newspaper staff work together, and all he said was that the groups had already been assigned. Then he said his lips were sealed, but he winked at me. So I bet you and I are in the same group."

"I hope so," Amy said.

On the far side of the bleachers, Dylan McKay sat alone at the end of a row. He didn't bother to look around at the other students; he had no special friends that he could hope to be paired with.

This situation was one Dylan had been dreading. It was bad enough always being compared with his brother, but at least Tom, a sixth grader, had always been in separate classes. Now they might have to work side by side, and everyone would see how inadequate Dylan was. Next to the talented Tom, Dylan was sure he would seem like even more of a dud than usual.

Dylan sat on the bench, shoulders hunched, head down, wishing he could just disappear.

In the front of the room, Mr. Bowman began to read out his list of names.

Jessica listened intently, but her name was not on the first list. She did hear her twin's name called and watched Elizabeth climb down from the bleachers and take her place in Mr. Bowman's group next to Amy Sutton. Jessica had stopped paying attention by the time Mr. Bowman got to the last name on his list.

"McKay," he announced.

"Hooray," one of the boys standing behind Mr. Bowman cheered, and several of the girls clapped. All eyes turned toward Tom, who was sitting in the front row, and he started to rise.

"That's *Dylan* McKay," Mr. Bowman corrected quickly.

Tom sat back down. The girls' smiles faded, and the boy who had cheered made a face.

"Oh no," he said, quite audibly.

Jessica saw the tall boy at the end of one of the rows stand up too quickly and teeter comically as he almost lost his balance. Then he caught himself and threaded his way down through the bleachers to the polished wooden floor, his face red.

Who can blame the group for booing, Jessica thought. *Who would want to work with him?*

Mr. Bowman motioned his group of students toward the other side of the gym, where they could talk more easily. Dylan walked slowly, lagging behind the rest of the kids.

Elizabeth had seen the unfortunate and very public snub the boy had received, and she felt a pang of sympathy.

"Come on," she whispered to Amy. "Let's say something nice to Dylan; he must feel awful!"

"Elizabeth," Amy pleaded. "Do you have to be nice to *everybody*?"

She followed her friend loyally but had to struggle to maintain her smile as Elizabeth slowed to match her steps to Dylan's.

"Hi," Elizabeth said, her smile sincere. "We're awfully glad to have you in our group."

Dylan stared at his feet as he shuffled across the smooth hardwood floor and hardly glanced at her.

"Yeah," he muttered.

Elizabeth, feeling rebuffed, tried again. *Maybe he's just shy,* she thought. She continued to walk beside him.

"I bet you'll be a big help to our company," she said. "We'll need some posters to advertise; do you draw?"

"No," Dylan muttered.

Elizabeth sighed. He seemed determined to rebuff her. But she wasn't ready to give up yet.

"We'll probably need to construct a booth or something. How are you in wood shop?"

Dylan shook his head, still refusing to meet her eyes. "Terrible. The only thing I ever managed to do in wood shop was almost cut off my finger," he told her glumly. "The teacher would hardly let me near the tools after that."

"Oh," Elizabeth answered, unable to think of an encouraging remark.

Amy, a few feet away, frowned and muttered to Elizabeth to join her.

"Well," Elizabeth said to the unfriendly boy, "I'm sure you'll think of something you enjoy doing."

He didn't answer. Elizabeth finally gave up and walked over to sit down beside Amy.

"Thank goodness," Amy hissed. "Why do you want to waste your time on that hermit? He doesn't like anybody!"

"I just hoped— Never mind." Elizabeth shook her head. "Let's see what Mr. Bowman has to tell us."

While the rest of the group settled on the bleachers and listened to the English teacher as he explained the project requirements, Dylan sat at the far edge of the group, too bitter to pay any attention to the assignment. What new disaster would follow this latest humiliation? No one wanted him here—he knew that for sure. Even the Wakefield girl, the only student in the group who had spoken to him, probably was waiting for him to make a fool of himself. His anger simmered inside like a bubbling pot of soup.

On the other side of the gym, Jessica still waited impatiently. Thank goodness the Hairnet hadn't read Jessica's name on her list, but several of the Unicorns had already been chosen. Lila looked increasingly skeptical, and Jessica could feel her reputation beginning to crumble.

Then Ms. Wyler, who was strict, but still more fun than Mrs. Arnette, began to read her list of names, and Jessica's was one of the first. She stood up quickly and winked at Lila.

"You'll be next," Jessica whispered, with renewed confidence that this project was going to work out the way she wanted it to.

And as if her confidence had proved the catalyst, Jessica wasn't even surprised to hear Lila's name called almost immediately. Then Ellen, Betsy Gordon, and Kimberly Haver, two seventh-grade Unicorns, followed in quick succession.

Jessica smiled broadly. This was going to work, after all. And to crown her happiness, she heard Tom McKay's name being called. The blond boy stood up with a weary expression, which he managed to make comical, and walked over to join the group. Jessica maneuvered herself to the edge of the cluster of students so she could smile sweetly at Tom as he joined them.

"Hi, Jessica," he said. "Are you ready to succeed in business?"

"I've got a great idea," she assured him. "Just wait till you hear. And you can be a big help."

She peered up at him through her long lashes and was pleased to see his blue eyes brighten in response.

Yes, this project was definitely going to be fun!

Five

◇

Jessica could hardly wait until Ms. Wyler finished her directions and allowed the students to discuss their ideas.

"What we should do," Jessica began confidently, "is start our own boutique."

"That's much too complicated," Kerry Glenn objected. "I think we should make pot holders. We did that in the third grade and sold lots of them."

"Pot holders?" Jessica could hardly contain her scorn. "That's for babies!"

"Jessica's right," Lila agreed. "How totally boring."

The other girl looked defensive. "We made lots of money for our third-grade classroom," she pointed out.

"Yes," Jessica told her. "Because our mothers

and grandmothers bought them all. But we have to sell this stuff within our own classes; that's one of the rules."

"Hey," one of the boys added. "What happens to the money we make?"

"We're using play money, don't you remember?" Jessica told him. "Each student starts out with twenty dollars to spend, and the company that makes the biggest profit at the end of the project period gets the highest grade and free sundaes at Casey's Place."

The boys cheered at the mention of the popular ice cream parlor in downtown Sweet Valley.

"All right!" Tom shouted.

"But I don't know, Jessica," Jerry McAllister said. "Boutiques are for girls; what would the boys do?"

Jessica thought quickly. She wanted the boys behind her. The whole group had to vote on the type of company they formed, and Jessica wasn't about to give up her great idea.

"We'll need a booth for the boutique. You guys can build it. And, of course, we'll sell some boys' stuff, too."

"I'd rather work on the booth, too," Mary Wallace, a seventh grader, spoke up. "And we have to make reports and financial statements and transportation schedules," she reminded them. "There'll be plenty for everyone to do."

Jessica looked a little surprised. It was beginning to sound like a lot of work to her, but she nodded generously. "Sure. Everyone will do his or her share. Come on, you guys, this will be fun."

"Why not?" Tom McKay agreed. "High fashion—look out, here we come!"

Jessica flashed a brilliant smile.

The students in Group C quickly voted in the boutique, and Jessica was feeling very pleased with herself.

"First we need to elect a president," she told the group. "Remember what Ms. Wyler said. We need someone who has good ideas and can lead the group." Jessica smiled at Tom again. "Do we have any nominations?"

Tom responded exactly as she hoped he would.

"I nominate Jessica Wakefield," he said loudly.

Lila seconded the nomination, and Jessica won easily.

She tried not to look too smug.

"Okay," she said in the best businesslike tone she could muster. "Let's get to work."

"Wait. We need some vice presidents, too," Lila prompted.

"That's right," Jessica agreed. "And since I'm president, I'll appoint them."

"Aren't we going to elect them?" one of the seventh graders asked.

"Nope," Jessica answered. "I'm president; it's part of my job to pick the vice presidents."

Some of the kids frowned, but Jessica didn't

take the time to notice. She couldn't even think about picking a vice president until she came up with a good company name.

"We'll call our company the Unicorn Boutique," she decided.

"Jessica," Lila pointed out, "not all the Unicorns are in this group. They'll feel bad at being left out."

"Hmmm." Jessica thought about that for a moment. "All right. What about the Purple Palace?" Purple was the Unicorns' favorite color. Jessica could just imagine the purple posters they could draw to advertise.

Jerry McAllister stuck out his tongue and made a thumbs down sign. "The pits," he said.

"Who asked you?" Jessica retorted, her expression indignant. Then, noting Ms. Wyler's frown, Jessica quickly smoothed her grimace into a peacemaker's smile.

"All right, Jerry, what's your suggestion?"

"Underwear from Outer Space." Jerry seemed so pleased with his brilliant suggestion that he almost fell off the bleachers laughing.

"Be serious," Jessica told him. "Tom, what do you think?"

"Since we're not selling space suits, I don't think Jerry's name is right," he said with a grin. "How about Sweet Valley Vogue?"

"Tom," Jessica cried, "that's brilliant!"

"My mother reads fashion magazines," Tom admitted, looking a little sheepish. "I always see them lying around the house."

All the girls in the group looked at him with admiration. "That's a great suggestion," Lila told him.

"Okay, let's move on to the next order of business," Jessica said, preferring that Tom keep his clear blue eyes focused on *her* and not wanting the group to forget who was in charge. "What do we need to do first?"

"We all have to go through our closets and collect clothes that we can give away to use for our inventory," Lila told them.

Jessica nodded in agreement.

"Then we'll sort them according to size," Kimberly Haver suggested, "and mark the prices on each item."

Jessica nodded. "That's good."

"I can see it now," Jerry snorted. "*Small, medium,* and *blimp*—that's for Lois Waller," he noted in a loud whisper.

"Come on, let's get back to business," Jessica told them, recalling how Elizabeth had once lectured her about making fun of people's weight problems.

Jessica was feeling very pleased with herself. She'd had no idea that being president of a company could be so much fun.

Across the gym, Elizabeth's group was arguing

about what kind of company to start. A couple of boys held out for slingshots.

"Don't be silly," Elizabeth told them. Even she was beginning to lose patience. "The school would never allow us to sell slingshots."

"What, then?" Amy demanded.

"I did have an idea." Elizabeth hesitated, a little uncertain of what the rest of her group would think about her plan.

"Don't tell me," Amy joked. "You want to open a stable and sell horses."

Several of the kids grinned. Elizabeth had once been obsessed with the idea of owning her own horse.

"Hey, that's not a bad idea," she said, "but what I have in mind will be a little easier to accomplish."

"What is it?" Olivia Davidson asked.

"What do you think of forming a publishing company and putting out a book of student writings?" Elizabeth's words came out in a rush because she was so afraid the other students wouldn't agree.

"You mean we'd have to do a lot of writing?" one of the boys objected, apparently afraid of doing any extra work.

"No, no," Elizabeth reassured him quickly. "We've got a bunch of writing to pick from already. Lots of kids have written essays for the big state contest. And we could ask students from other groups to contribute stories and poems they've already written. We'd have plenty of material to use."

"'But how do we print a book?" Nora Mercandy asked. "We don't have any printing equipment."

"I know," Elizabeth agreed. "But we have the typewriter the newspaper staff uses. If we type up the pages very neatly, I bet Mr. Bowman would help us duplicate them. Then, all we have to do is draw illustrations, staple the books together, and put covers on them. We could make a great book!"

The rest of the students began to catch Elizabeth's enthusiasm. She glanced over at their interested faces, hesitating only when she caught sight of Dylan McKay frowning in the back of the group.

What is wrong with that boy? she asked herself.

Six

◇

Dylan McKay sat slumped on the edge of the bleachers, as far removed from the rest of the group as he could get without attracting attention. *Of all the dumb luck*, he thought, glancing across the gym to where his brother stood surrounded by friends. Why did they have to put the sixth and seventh grades together for this project? If there was any advantage Dylan had over Tom, it was being a year ahead of him, both in age and in school. Dylan, by rights, should be the brother more skilled in sports, more poised in social situations. But no, it was Tom who excelled, Tom whom everyone liked.

Dylan saw Elizabeth Wakefield glance at him as the group continued to discuss their book ideas. He looked away so he wouldn't have to meet her gaze. No one would want to know what *he* thought. Elizabeth probably wished that Tom was sitting here instead of Dummy Dylan.

He looked across the gymnasium again and watched Tom in the center of a group of excited students, all trying to talk at once as they planned their company.

The vague pain inside Dylan turned sharp, like a knife twisting in his stomach. Biting his lip, he fought with himself, determined not to show the other students how he felt.

One of the boys on the bench below him looked up and said, "Dylan, do you . . ." But at the sight of Dylan's scowl, the boy hesitated.

"What?" Dylan grunted.

"Do you know how to use a hammer?"

Dylan shook his head.

The other seventh grader turned quickly to the boy next to him.

No one likes me, Dylan thought. *If Tom weren't here, maybe I'd have a chance.*

Later, after the teacher had dismissed them for lunch, the ugly thought persisted. Dylan, walking slowly toward his locker, repeated to himself, *If it weren't for Tom . . .*

He took his time exchanging notebooks at his locker, hoping to get to the lunchroom late so he could avoid most of the other students. Instead, when he walked into the big, sunny room, Dylan saw Tom waiting a few feet from the doorway.

"Hey, Dylan. What kind of company is your

group dreaming up?" he asked as he approached. "We're going into high fashion. Can you believe it?"

Tom grinned at his brother, waiting for a response.

Dylan just stood there staring at the denim backpack that his brother was carrying.

"That's my backpack," Dylan said, his voice hard. "What are you doing with it?"

Typical, Dylan thought, still staring blindly at the backpack, not noticing Tom's surprised expression. *Tom gets everything from attention right on down to my possessions.* The anger inside Dylan exploded. When he glanced up, his fierce expression seemed to startle his brother.

"I guess I picked up the wrong bag this morning," Tom explained. "Sorry."

Dylan hardly noticed the apology. The anger inside him was too strong. He grabbed the backpack so hard that one of the books fell out.

Tom put out his hand.

"Let me take my books out first, will you?"

"You just think you can do anything you want, don't you?" Dylan sneered.

Tom blinked, and his face darkened. "Come on, Dylan," he said. "What are you getting so upset about?"

Dylan dropped the backpack that had started the dispute. Throwing around the bag didn't vent his anger. He wanted more.

"Who says I'm upset?" he demanded. He stepped forward and gave his brother a shove.

Tom, caught by surprise, lost his balance and fell backward into the middle of a group of students seated at a long table. Unable to catch himself, he jostled one girl, then hit the table. Several of the girls shrieked in alarm as their food spilled and slid across the tabletop.

Tom, regaining his footing, turned to look at Elizabeth Wakefield. She had been about to take a sip of milk and now stared in surprise. The carton in her hand had been jolted; chocolate milk spotted her clothes.

"Watch out!" Elizabeth cried.

Seven

◇

Elizabeth had hardly uttered her warning when Dylan McKay's lanky form lunged forward again.

Tom swung around, but not soon enough. Dylan's clumsy punch hit him in the stomach and he doubled over.

"No fair!" Amy yelled.

Elizabeth, who had been talking to Amy and Julie Porter about their newly formed publishing company, sat wide-eyed, still in shock from Tom's body catapulting into their midst. Amy had dropped the apple she was eating, then watched in dismay as it rolled under the next lunch table. Julie had dropped her sandwich and screamed.

Now Tom, trying to stand upright, brought up his arms in an attempt to protect himself. Dylan continued to swing at him. Several boys edged forward, then hesitated.

Dylan was the taller McKay, but he lacked the athletic ability and strength of his younger brother. Tom stepped out of reach as Dylan swung wildly.

"Dylan," he cried. "What's the matter with you?"

Dylan's face was red, his mouth drawn into a grim line. He didn't answer.

"I don't want to fight with you," Tom told him.

Although his tone was low, the students around them heard, and everyone looked shocked.

"Why's that jerk picking on his own brother?" Julie demanded.

Elizabeth suddenly remembered the conversation she had heard between the McKay brothers. She had the feeling she might understand more about this one-sided fight than the other kids. Elizabeth shook her head. Dylan wasn't doing himself any good this way.

"Leave Tom alone," Jerry McAllister called out.

"Pick on someone your own size!" one of the other boys added.

But Dylan ignored them all. "Come on," he urged his brother. "Hit me!"

But Tom obviously didn't want to fight. Instead of raising his fists, he held out one hand toward his brother, palm up. "Let's talk about it," he said quietly.

"Fight, darn it!" Dylan grunted. He swung again, almost knocking his round glasses off his nose. Again Tom stepped out of harm's way. But this only seemed to make Dylan's anger grow.

"What's the matter." He spat out the words. "Chicken?"

Tom's expression hardened. "This is really dumb, Dylan," he said. "I don't even know what you're mad about."

At that moment, Dylan lunged forward, and his fist connected with his brother's face with a force that surprised them both.

"Oh, no," Julie shrieked.

Elizabeth caught her breath, watching the red drops begin to appear at the end of Tom's nose. Even Dylan looked shaken.

"That's enough!" Jerry yelled. He hurried to step between the brothers, and Charlie Cashman followed. "Go pick on someone else, you bully."

Dylan, who had been flushed with anger, now looked pale. He glanced toward his brother and seemed about to speak. But instead, he slowly headed for the door, head down.

Elizabeth handed a clean paper napkin to Tom and then watched Dylan disappear through the doorway. He got away just in time, too, she thought. Mr. Bowman was quickly making his way across the lunchroom toward them.

"What's going on here?" the teacher demanded.

Tom, wiping his nose, was the first to answer.

"Nothing," he told the teacher. "I slipped and hit my nose on the table, that's all. It's not bleeding much."

Mr. Bowman's brows lifted. "Better go down to the nurse and let her take a look at it. And no more *accidents*," he said, flashing Tom a meaningful look.

"Yes, sir," Tom said.

Jerry waited until the teacher walked away, then said, "You want me to go with you? Just wait, we'll get Dylan!"

Tom shook his head. "No," he said quietly. "It's okay. Dylan and I will work it out."

He shrugged and walked toward the door, still holding the napkin to his nose. The other students watched him go, then turned back to their lunch.

"That Dylan is really awful," Amy said loudly, still hungry for her lost apple. "I wish we'd gotten Tom in our group instead of him."

Elizabeth looked down at her good blue sweater. Drops of chocolate milk stained the knit fabric. She shook her head and said thoughtfully, "I think Dylan may have his reasons."

"Not for acting like that," Julie argued. "I can't believe we're stuck with him in our group, Elizabeth. Can't we complain to the teachers?"

"Let's give him a chance," Elizabeth begged. "Sometimes people do strange things when they're unhappy. Remember how wrong we were about

Brooke Dennis? She acted like a world-class snob when she first moved to Sweet Valley. The whole school conspired against her—"

"Oh, yes." Amy giggled. "That was the time you and Jessica pretended to have another sister, a triplet."

Elizabeth shuddered. "Don't remind me," she said. "But anyway, when we discovered that Brooke acted so badly just because she was unhappy over her parents' divorce, it explained a lot of things. And Brooke turned out to be a lot of fun."

"But the McKays aren't divorced," Amy argued, still reluctant to give the belligerent Dylan the benefit of the doubt. "Dylan doesn't have any problems at home."

Elizabeth looked straight at Julie and Amy. "There are lots of different kinds of problems."

The other girls didn't seem convinced. "I still think he's a total psycho," Amy declared.

"Me, too," Julie said.

Elizabeth sighed. Dylan was going to be a complete outcast if he continued to act like this.

Eight

◇

For the rest of the day, the whole middle school talked about nothing but the fight between the McKay brothers. Even before lunch period ended, the news had spread through the hallways.

"Can you imagine," Betsy Gordon, a seventh grader, exclaimed to the small group of girls clustered around her. "That awful Dylan practically *murdered* his own brother!"

Jessica nodded vigorously. "Elizabeth saw the whole thing; Dylan spilled chocolate milk all over one of her best sweaters. And I was going to borrow it tomorrow," she concluded with a sigh. "I bet Dylan did it on purpose."

"It was awful," Mary Wallace agreed. "I wish Tom was in the seventh grade instead of Dylan."

"Kimberly Haver *did* invite Tom to her birthday

party next Friday, didn't she?" Jessica asked. She was anxious to spend more time with Tom. He was bound to notice her charms if she gave him sufficient opportunity.

"Of course," Tamara Chase assured her. "She invited the best kids from the sixth grade—"

"Good." Jessica nodded, sure that she and her sister would have to be included in that description.

"And everyone in the seventh grade," Tamara finished. "Well, *almost* everyone."

The girls exchanged glances. No one had to point out which unpopular seventh grader just might have been *accidentally* overlooked.

"It's going to be a super party," Betsy said. "Kimberly has a whole stack of new records, and her dad is renting strobe lights to put up in their rec room."

The bell signalling the next class interrupted these pleasant thoughts, and the girls hurried off in different directions.

Meanwhile, Elizabeth was thinking not of the upcoming party, but about her group's company, of which she had been elected president. She wanted their book to be really impressive, not just for the grade, but because Elizabeth truly loved books.

So when some of the members of the "Sweet Valley Publishing Company" began to trickle into the newspaper room after school, she quickly put them to work.

"Amy," Elizabeth said, "you sit down with this stack of student writings and decide which ones you think we should pick. And remember, we want to use as many as possible."

"Wow," Amy said, tossing her stringy blond hair back over her shoulder. She took the large stack of papers. "Did Sweet Valley students really write all this?"

Elizabeth nodded. "It's because of the big state essay contest," she reminded her best friend. "We had a lot of entries, and Mr. Bowman said it would be all right to publish some of them in our booklet."

Just then two more girls came into the room. "Here's the poetry you wanted to see," Lois Waller said shyly, holding out several sheets of paper.

"Thanks, Lois." Elizabeth smiled at the stout girl.

"Are you really going to print them in your book?" Lois looked very impressed.

"I can't say until I see how many submissions we get, but we'll try to use at least one."

As more members of the publishing company filtered in, Elizabeth quickly thought of assignments for them. "Ronnie, you and Randy can start building a display case to sell our books when they're printed. There are some cardboard boxes in the closet Mr. Bowman said we could use, and some poster paint to decorate them. Olivia, you can start work on some illustrations; you're so good at drawing."

Olivia smiled. She took a seat at one of the empty desks, and the boys went to the closet and pulled out the supplies. Soon everyone was hard at work, with only occasional joking and giggling, and Elizabeth, looking through a stack of essays, became thoroughly absorbed in her reading. Then a sudden silence warned her that something was wrong. Elizabeth looked around the room. Everyone had stopped his work to stare at the door. Elizabeth turned quickly to see Dylan McKay standing in the doorway, his expression defiant.

"You said to come by after school." He spoke directly to Elizabeth, seeming to ignore the hostile glances from the other students.

Elizabeth's sympathy overcame her earlier anger. Looking into his troubled brown eyes, Elizabeth suspected that Dylan was more unhappy than anyone knew. And he *had* come to work, as she had asked.

She put down her stack of papers and tried to think of a job to give Dylan that wouldn't risk his being snubbed by the other kids.

"Let me see. Where do we need another worker most?" Elizabeth asked herself aloud. Looking at Dylan, she asked, "Can you type?"

"A little," he said.

"Good," Elizabeth said. Typing was the one thing he could do all by himself. "Take these essays Amy and I have already read; they'll probably be approved for final inclusion in our book. You can start typing a clean copy of each one."

Dylan nodded and followed Elizabeth to the beat-up typewriter that the newspaper staff used. He dropped his books on the table beside the typewriter, pulled up a chair, and took the stack of papers from Elizabeth.

Olivia, who was closest to Dylan, glanced at him from the corner of her eye and shifted her chair a little farther away. The two boys building the display case turned their backs on him.

Elizabeth sighed. But Dylan, although the tips of his ears had turned suspiciously red, was hunched over the typewriter and he didn't show that he'd noticed.

Everyone settled down to work again, but the feeling of easy camaraderie had been lost. No one giggled or joked; instead everyone worked in silence, with occasional whispers and glances at Dylan.

Even Elizabeth found it difficult to concentrate. She found herself having to reread the pages in her hand several times, and she still didn't know what she'd read.

Oh no, Elizabeth thought. *Is one boy going to ruin our whole project?*

Fortunately, Olivia looked up just then at the clock on the wall and exclaimed, "Oh, it's four-thirty already. I have to go, Elizabeth."

"Okay. Thanks for coming," Elizabeth said, taking the pictures the other girl handed her. "These are really good, Olivia. They'll look great in the book!"

Olivia blushed, and her face lit up with a smile.

The other kids also got up to leave. Ronnie showed Elizabeth how they'd constructed the frame for the display case. "We'll paint it tomorrow," he told her.

"You guys did a great job," Elizabeth said approvingly.

"Good thing one of us knows what we're doing," Randy said, glancing toward Dylan, who still sat hunched over the typewriter. The slow clatter of the typewriter keys had already revealed to Elizabeth that Dylan's typing was not very good, but she kept her expression even.

"Thanks, Randy," she said quickly. "I'll see you both tomorrow."

She turned from the boys to a group of girls who were also leaving, and by the time Elizabeth had collected all the papers and turned back to her own desk, she noticed that Dylan Mckay had slipped out of the room without even saying good-bye.

Had he done any work at all? Elizabeth walked over to the typewriter to take a look. A piece of typing paper remained in the old typewriter, and the portion of the essay that Dylan had typed revealed several mistakes, some of them messily erased and typed over.

Elizabeth shook her head. Dylan had said he could type a little. Boy, was that an understatement. She'd have to retype a lot of it.

Amy, who was waiting for her, saw the expression on Elizabeth's face and asked, "What's wrong?"

"Not only did Dylan *not* type the essays," Elizabeth said, exasperated, "but he's gotten some of his own papers mixed up with the ones I gave him. Look, here's an old math work sheet."

Amy giggled at the disgust in Elizabeth's tone. "What did you expect—giving an important job to that guy? Maybe if we speak to Mr. Bowman, we can persuade him to move Dylan to another group. We don't want him messing up our project."

Elizabeth's anger was already fading. "We can't do that, Amy. It would hurt his feelings. Besides, you know that none of the other groups will want him, either. And he has to work on one of the companies. Come on. I'll finish this typing at home."

They walked outside, and Elizabeth spotted Jessica and Lila loitering on the school lawn, talking to Tom McKay. Jessica's blue-green eyes sparkled as she turned on her considerable charm.

As Elizabeth and Amy approached, Tom suddenly glanced at his watch.

"I've got to run," he told the girls. "See you tomorrow."

"Hi, Jess," Elizabeth called to her sister. "Ready to walk home?"

Jessica nodded.

"See you tomorrow, Jessica," Lila drawled.

Amy walked with the Wakefield twins for a couple of blocks, then turned down her own street. "Bye, Jessica. See you, Elizabeth," she said. "Our book is going to turn out great; I just know we'll have the best project of all."

As the twins walked on alone, Elizabeth couldn't resist teasing her sister. "I suppose you were talking to Tom McKay about your student company?"

Jessica grinned. "Of course," she assured her sister, her expression innocent. "Doesn't he have the bluest eyes you've ever seen? I told him how awful I thought it was that Dylan picked on him at lunch."

"What did he say?" Elizabeth asked.

"He said it wasn't his brother's fault, but I don't believe that for a minute. After all, Lizzie, you were there. You saw the whole thing."

"Yes." Elizabeth nodded. "But I still wonder why Dylan did it."

"Who cares?" Jessica tossed her long blond hair and dismissed Dylan as too boring for further comment. "But Tom is a dream; he's working hard on our boutique. And we're going to have some great clothes to sell, not to mention scarfs and bracelets and all. I might even buy something myself."

"So what else is new?" Elizabeth giggled.

"Well, our book is going to be really good."

"That's nice," Jessica agreed vaguely, her mind

on more important matters. "There's this purple blouse that Tamara outgrew that would look really good on me, Lizzie."

Elizabeth resigned herself to listening to a detailed rundown of the clothing possibilities for the rest of their walk home.

Nine

When the twins arrived home, Mrs. Wakefield called out, "About time, you two! Hurry and get the table set—dinner's almost ready."

"Okay, Mom," Elizabeth said, hurrying upstairs to put her books in her room. She came back downstairs to find Jessica talking to her mother.

"I'm doing a great job on the project," Jessica was saying. "You and Dad are really going to be proud of me."

"I'm proud already that you're putting so much time and work into it," Mrs. Wakefield assured her daughter, pausing to give her a quick hug. "I'm glad that you took our family discussion to heart this time. I knew you could improve your efforts at school, Jessica."

Elizabeth, observing Jessica's smug expression,

couldn't help feeling just a little skeptical. She suspected that Jessica's new enthusiasm for her school
project had something to do with her determination
not to be grounded before Kimberly's birthday party.
On the other hand, being able to work her project
around a subject dear to her heart seemed to have
done wonders for Jessica's motivation.

Jessica chattered about her boutique all the way
through dinner.

"Leave it to Jessica," Steven observed, shaking
his head. "Turning a school project into a clothes
fair."

"At least I have some sense of style," Jessica told
him. "That's more than can be said for *you*. What
about that striped shirt you wore to school today?
Yuck!"

"I'll have you know that Gloria Andrews said I
looked cool," Steven retorted. His face slowly turned
red when he realized what he had just said.

"Gloria, huh?" Jessica observed. "I guess we
know who Steven likes!"

"I do not. She's just a girl I know," Steven muttered, trying to hide his red face behind his glass of
milk.

"How is your project coming, Elizabeth?" Mr.
Wakefield asked, tactfully changing the subject.

"Fine, Dad," Elizabeth told him. "Our book is
going to be a real literary masterpiece!"

Steven choked over his glass of milk. "That'll be
the day." He laughed, forgetting his own embarrass-

ment. "I can see it now—Elizabeth Wakefield, the Shakespeare of the sixth grade!"

Elizabeth threw him an injured look. "It'll be a *good* book," she insisted. "We have some of the student essays written for the state contest, and some poetry. . . ."

"Poetry? That's boring," Jessica said. "Too bad you're not publishing a fashion magazine. That would have been interesting."

Elizabeth groaned.

"Well, I can't wait for the sports banquet Friday night. Our coach will be announcing the trophy winners for the season, and then we'll be getting our letters!"

"That's wonderful, Steven," Mr. Wakefield said.

"We can't wait to see you receive your letter," Mrs. Wakefield continued.

"Friday?" Jessica suddenly reentered the conversation. "Lila and I were planning to go to the twilight show at the Valley Cinema; there's a new movie that everyone says is really good."

"I think Steven's sports banquet is a bit more important," Mrs. Wakefield told her, while Steven nodded vigorously. "You can go to the show with Lila another time."

"But I already promised her!" Jessica protested.

"Sorry, Jessica," Mrs. Wakefield said firmly. "Friday night we're all going to be at the banquet honoring Steven and his team."

Jessica pushed back her plate and stood up. "I guess I know who's important in this family!" She stormed off toward the stairs.

"Really, Jessica," her mother murmured, frowning at the sudden display of temper.

Steven grinned. "That's okay," he said. "I'll eat her dessert."

Elizabeth, despite a twinge of sympathy for her sister, couldn't help giggling.

After dinner, Elizabeth went up to her room. Fortunately, she didn't have a lot of homework. She wanted to do more reading of entries for the book, but first she had to sort out the mess Dylan had made of the student papers.

She removed several crumpled sheets of Dylan's old homework from the stack of essays, and then paused at another paper.

Elizabeth began to read the scribbled words. "Freedom of speech is one of the quiet freedoms that we sometimes forget that we enjoy. Only when it is lost, when books are burned, when newspapers are silenced, when the ordinary person's right to speak his or her mind without fear is taken away, do we remember what a precious part of our heritage freedom of speech really is."

Wow, this is really good! Elizabeth thought. *Is this one of the essays?*

She looked over the paper again, searching in vain for the author's name. This was undoubtedly one of the contest essays, and it was certainly the best one she had read. Even better than her own entry, Elizabeth thought fairly.

Suddenly Elizabeth drew a deep breath. The handwriting was familiar! In fact, she had just seen samples of it. Afraid to trust her memory, Elizabeth grabbed the wastebasket in which Dylan McKay's old homework papers lay. She grabbed a tattered sheet of science questions and compared the handwriting on the two papers.

There was no doubt in her mind. This essay had been written by Dylan McKay.

But why hadn't he mentioned it? A terrible thought struck her. Had Dylan forgotten to mail his essay in? The deadline was so close!

She grabbed the essay and hurried to the phone in the hallway. Thumbing through the phone book, she soon located the McKay number and dialed.

To her relief, it was Dylan who answered.

"Dylan, I wanted to speak to you. You got some of your papers mixed up with the sheets you were typing this afternoon."

"Oh," he said. "I'm sorry."

"That's okay," Elizabeth assured him. "But, Dylan, I found your entry for the big state essay contest. You've got to get it in the mail tonight or it will be disqualified!"

There was a long silence at the other end of the line, then Dylan said, "It doesn't matter. Throw it away."

The line went dead. Elizabeth stared at the receiver in her hand, shocked. Throw away this great essay? He must be kidding.

She replaced the receiver slowly and sat down on her bed, still holding Dylan's paper. What should she do? She couldn't throw away an essay as good as this one.

She sat in silence for several minutes, worrying over the problem, when a solution came to her. She could enter the essay for him!

Then Elizabeth bit her lip. Would that be right? She jumped off her bed and began to pace up and down.

"What's the matter?" Jessica said, sticking her head through the doorway. "I'm trying to read the latest issue of *Ingenue*. Will you quit stomping around?"

"Sorry," Elizabeth murmured, too deep in thought to pay attention to her twin. Abruptly, she made up her mind. Hurrying to her desk, Elizabeth flipped through her notebook, finding the flyer with the address for the contest entries. She quickly made up a proper title page for Dylan's essay, stuffed it all in an envelope, and added a stamp. Then she grabbed her jacket and ran for the stairs.

"Hey, where are you going?" Jessica yelled after her twin.

"I've got to get Mom to drive me to the post office," Elizabeth called. "That's the only way to get this letter postmarked by the deadline."

"Oh." Jessica quickly lost interest and disappeared back into her bedroom.

Elizabeth explained the situation to her mother, then finished addressing the envelope in the car as they sped toward Sweet Valley's main post office.

As Mrs. Wakefield pulled into the big parking lot, Elizabeth could only ask herself, was she doing the right thing?

Ten

◇

On Thursday morning Jessica and Elizabeth walked to school together as usual. Jessica chattered away about the clothes soon to be on display in the boutique. Elizabeth pretended to listen to her sister, but deep inside, she still wondered if she'd done the right thing.

Surely Dylan will forgive me, Elizabeth told herself.

"Don't you agree?" Jessica's voice interrupted her thoughts.

"What?" Elizabeth tried to pull her attention back to the moment.

"I said, don't you think that two vice presidents are enough?" Jessica repeated. "I've already appointed Lila and Kimberly. Lila's my best friend in the group, and Kimberly invited me to her party. But now Tamara and Betsy want to be vice presidents, too." Jessica sounded gloomy. Being president of a company was turning out to be more trouble than it was worth.

"If you explain that you have enough vice presidents already, surely they'll understand," Elizabeth said, trying not to giggle at Jessica's reasoning.

"I hope so." Jessica sighed. She brightened as she caught sight of several of her friends waiting by the side door. "See you later, Lizzie."

"See you, Jess." Elizabeth waved to her sister and hurried into school, anxious to find Amy.

Meanwhile Jessica walked into school at a more leisurely pace, accompanied by Lila and Ellen.

"I brought some more clothes for our boutique, Jessica," Lila said, nodding toward a bundle Ellen carried in her arms.

"Good." Jessica nodded. "That will give us an even bigger inventory."

"I don't understand why vice presidents can't carry their own packages," Ellen said with a sigh.

Jessica looked surprised, but when she turned to Lila, the other girl shrugged.

"Jessica did say that presidents and vice presidents are *executive* positions," she pointed out, a bit smugly.

"Aren't executives allowed to work?" Ellen wondered.

Fortunately the first bell rang, and Jessica didn't have to think of an answer.

"Come on," she told the others. "Let's take this clothing and leave it with our other stuff in Ms. Wyler's closet."

They deposited their bundles and hurried off to class.

The last two periods of the day were devoted to work on the student companies, and Jessica and the rest of her group gathered in Ms. Wyler's room.

"Jessica," Tamara said as soon as the group had assembled. "Did you think about what I said—about making me vice president?"

"Well . . ." Jessica stalled, trying to remember what Elizabeth had told her to say. "I don't really think we need any more vice presidents."

"That's not fair," Tamara complained. "I have some really good ideas about displaying our clothing."

"Oh, all right," Jessica said. She was bored with Tamara's complaints and decided it would be easier to give in. "You can be vice president in charge of displays."

"What about me?" Betsy complained. "How come Tamara gets to be a vice president and I don't?"

"We don't need . . ." Jessica began, then sighed. "Oh, forget it. You can be vice president in charge of—of supervision."

"What does that mean?" Betsy asked, apparently afraid that Tamara had been given a better title than she had.

"It just means that you have to come up with good ideas, too," Jessica explained quickly.

"What about us?" Charlie Cashman complained. "We're doing all the work putting up the booth; shouldn't we be vice presidents too?"

"Fine!" Jessica threw up her hands. "You're both vice presidents in charge of construction."

Satisfied, the two boys went back to the booth, and the rest of the group gathered in a circle to discuss how to manage their boutique.

"These clothes probably should be sorted by size, don't you think?" Tamara suggested. "And we have to put a price on all of them and set up our cashier's box for the money we'll collect. Do we have to add sales tax when we sell our things?"

"I'm afraid so," Lila moaned. "Who's good at math?"

"Not me," Jessica said. "Betsy and Tom can work on that, and Lila and I will start some posters to advertise our boutique. We have to let our customers know what we're selling. Then we still haven't done the transportation schedules or the financial statements."

"Vice presidents don't have to do that stuff," Lila scoffed.

Jessica frowned at her friend.

"I'm a vice president, too," Tamara objected. She had begun sorting clothes, but now she pushed the garments aside.

"So am I!" Betsy said.

"Now wait a minute," Jessica begged. She had a feeling things were getting out of hand.

"Oh Jessica, let's take a break," Lila suggested.

Jessica, feeling that she had lost control, nodded. The students wandered off into smaller groups, talking and giggling among themselves.

"Are we still going to the show Friday night?" Lila asked.

Jessica's expression darkened. "No," she said. "We all have to go to Steven's stupid sports banquet."

"Gosh," Lila said. "That's terrible."

"I can't wait for Kimberly's party. Do you think her basement is big enough to hold all the kids she's invited?" Jessica brightened, thinking of the treat in store. "Maybe Tom McKay will ask me to dance."

"He's a dream, isn't he?" Lila said.

"Who?" Ellen demanded, coming to sit down beside them.

Jessica blushed, glancing across the room to see if Tom might have overheard, too. Lila whispered an answer to Ellen's question. Ellen giggled.

The next two hours went by very quickly, and when Ms. Wyler returned to the room to check on her group, she found everyone talking and laughing.

Ms. Wyler looked stern. "How many posters have you drawn?" she asked.

Lila looked slightly embarrassed. "We've got one almost finished," she told the teacher.

"In two hours you've only done one poster?"

Ms. Wyler didn't look impressed. "Did you get all your clothing sorted and priced; did you begin the reports?"

Jessica, who knew that they'd hardly begun, tried not to look guilty. "Almost," she assured the teacher, while she thought, *How did the time go by so quickly? At least the booth is finished.*

But when Jessica turned to survey the rest of the group's handiwork, she found the cardboard booth still unpainted. The construction committee had stopped their work and were discussing the newest video game at the mall.

"Jessica," Ms. Wyler said. "Being president means you have to make sure that the work gets done."

Jessica flushed. *Really,* she thought indignantly. *Is it my fault they can't keep their mind on their work?*

When the last bell rang, Jessica found Elizabeth waiting on the school lawn.

"How's your company doing?" Elizabeth asked. She smiled at her twin. "We got lots of work done today; I'm so excited about our book. I can't wait 'til it's ready."

"Oh, be quiet," Jessica wailed.

"What's wrong?" Elizabeth gazed at her twin with concern.

"We didn't get much work done," Jessica admitted. "I gave everybody the titles they wanted, and we still don't seem to be making progress."

"That's bad, Jess," Elizabeth said, worried.

"Mom and Dad are counting on you getting a good grade."

"I know!" Jessica moaned. "And I thought being president would be so much fun, but it's not. It's just more to worry about!"

They walked home slowly. At dinner, when the Wakefield family was gathered around the dining table, Mr. Wakefield asked the same question.

"How are my budding capitalists doing?" he asked.

Jessica looked down at her plate.

Elizabeth, sensing her sister's reluctance to answer, hurried to reply. "Great, Dad. My group agreed on which of the student writings to use, and we got over half of them typed today. Tomorrow we'll finish typing the poems and essays, and Mr. Bowman will help us duplicate them on Monday. Then we can put them together and start selling our book. We're calling the book *Sweet Valley Journal*."

"Sounds terrific," Mr. Wakefield said. "I can't wait to read it. And how about your group, Jessica?"

Jessica still stared at her plate. "We're doing great, too," she mumbled. Then, suddenly afraid that her whole wonderful idea was going to come tumbling down around her, she admitted, "Well, it'll probably turn out all right. But we've had a few problems."

Jessica felt better after that. She sat up straighter and met her father's gaze. He looked concerned but not angry.

"What's the problem?"

"For one thing, everyone wanted to be a vice president," Jessica explained. "So I promoted Lila, Betsy, Tamara, Kimberly, and Jerry. But then, when Ms. Wyler asked about the reports and financial statements and transportation graphs we have to make, they all said that vice presidents don't have to do that work. That's for the rest of the company."

Steven gave a hoot of laughter. "Some president you are," he croaked. "Your company sounds like an upside-down pyramid."

Mr. Wakefield smiled. "I'm afraid Steven has a point. Sounds like you've got more chiefs than Indians."

"What does that mean?" Jessica wanted to know.

"It means there are more leaders than followers," her father explained. "The more important your title, the more responsibility you have. You should have discovered that already. Being president means you have to oversee all the workers and make sure they get their jobs done, even the vice presidents!"

Jessica nodded. "Being president of the company isn't as much fun as I expected," she confessed. "What am I going to do?"

"Make all your vice presidents get to work," her father told her. "And set a good example by doing a fair share of the work yourself."

Jessica, frowning a little at this advice, nodded

reluctantly. "I guess I have to," she agreed, ignoring Steven's chuckles.

"Jessica working! The middle school may never recover from the shock," Steven murmured beneath his breath.

Jessica shot him an angry look. "You just wait and see," she said.

The next day Jessica was true to her word. "No joking around today," she told the other kids. "We're going to get this work done. I want the booth painted, the posters finished, the clothes all sorted and priced, the cash box ready, and the reports and graphs at least started. And *everyone* works!"

"I can't paint," Lila objected. "I don't want to get all messy."

"Then you can sort clothes," Jessica told her.

Lila pouted, but she sat down with the bundles.

Under Jessica's unrelenting supervision, the students in her group finished their booth, sorted out most of the clothes, and by the end of the day had drawn half a dozen posters advertising their wares.

Elizabeth discovered Jessica taping the last poster to the wall at the end of the main hallway.

"There you are," Elizabeth exclaimed. "I've been looking all over for you."

"I had to put up our posters," Jessica told her twin, feeling important. "We want everyone to know what great stuff we'll have to sell next week."

Elizabeth inspected the poster. "It looks good, Jess."

"Thanks." Jessica grinned. "I'm glad they're all done, though. Now I've got to work on this dumb transportation schedule. Think maybe you could give me some help?" She looked at her sister hopefully.

"I've got work of my own to do, I'm afraid," Elizabeth pointed out. "Since I'm good at math, my group insisted that I do the financial report."

"We have to do one of those, too," Jessica said. "But luckily Tom McKay said he'd do it. You can't do very much until you know how many books you've sold, Lizzie."

"That's true." Elizabeth looked pleased at Jessica's knowledge. "My company has to pay for our paper, and the copying, then put down how many copies we sell, and figure out our profits after the expenses are deducted. I never knew business was so complicated!"

"Me, either," Jessica agreed. "But, about this transportation schedule . . ."

Elizabeth laughed. "You never give up, do you?" she said, but her tone was affectionate. How often had Jessica wheedled her twin into helping her out? But Elizabeth didn't really mind. "Okay, I'll help you, but you've got to pick up a bus or train schedule yourself."

"Good grief," Jessica moaned. "When can I get one?"

Elizabeth gave the question some thought. "I know," she said. "When Mom drives me over to the stables for my riding lesson tomorrow, she can take you to the bus station afterwards and you can pick up a schedule."

"Oh, all right," Jessica grumbled. "But I was supposed to go over to Lila's. It's bad enough I had to cancel my plans with her tonight just to sit through that sports banquet!"

Elizabeth looked shocked. "Aren't you proud of Steven's achievements, too?" she asked her sister. "I'm sure you'll have a good time. Besides, there'll probably be lots of cute high school boys there."

"That's true." Jessica perked up. "Maybe I'll get to see Josh."

Elizabeth shook her head. Jessica's secret, brief romance with the sixteen-year-old had gotten her into loads of trouble.

"Just remember . . ."

"I'm just going to say hello," Jessica said quickly, to avoid a lecture. "Let's go home."

"Not before you check your locker," Elizabeth said.

"What for?" Jessica demanded, puzzled by her sister's mysterious smile.

"You'll see."

Jessica turned and hurried down the hall to her locker, followed by Elizabeth. Jessica twirled the combination lock and pulled open the door. When a bright red envelope fell out, Jessica pounced on it.

"What is it?"

"Open it, silly." Elizabeth laughed. "I got mine already. It's the invitation to Kimberly's party. I knew you'd be excited."

"Oh, I already knew we'd be invited," Jessica said with a superior tone, but she still smiled at the sight of the envelope.

"Well, I didn't," Elizabeth admitted. "Kimberly told Amy that she hadn't invited many sixth graders, though she asked *all* of the seventh graders. Her mother insisted."

"It's going to be a great party," Jessica exclaimed. "I can't wait!"

Eleven

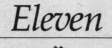

Dylan McKay walked home alone, shuffling his feet along the dusty sidewalk as he reviewed his disastrous day. It had started just before lunch. When Dylan walked into the cafeteria, the kids standing in the lunch line had all been talking about one thing: Kimberly Haver's party.

Dylan hardly knew Kimberly, so at first he had thought little about it. But when he took his tray and sat down at a table in the back of the lunchroom, the kids sitting at the other end were also discussing the party.

And then, after school, while he was opening the combination lock on his locker he heard another knot of seventh graders laughing together and talking about what kinds of presents they were going to get for Kimberly.

"Isn't it great?" Betsy Gordon exclaimed. "This is going to be the best party of the whole year."

The other kids nodded.

"Yeah, and *everyone* is going to be there. Kimberly invited the whole seventh grade, and a few sixth graders," Tamara Chase said. "I can't wait!"

Nobody noticed that Dylan was listening, but he heard their words clearly. He turned the knob on his locker slowly, reluctant to look inside.

When Dylan swung open the metal door, a rush of bitterness overwhelmed him. Inside he saw his familiar battered books, an old magazine, some dirty gym clothes. But there was no invitation awaiting him.

So what else is new? he thought angrily. *Who would want me at a party? What do I care?*

But he did care. He kept hearing Tamara's voice saying, "Kimberly invited the *whole* seventh grade."

This was the last straw!

The more he thought about how the whole seventh grade class had been invited, the darker Dylan's mood became.

When he finally walked up the driveway of the McKay home, he saw his brother, Tom, tennis racket in hand, practicing his swings by hitting a tennis ball against the garage wall.

"Hi," his younger brother called. "How did your group go?"

Dylan shrugged. "Okay."

"Ready for the big event?"

"What?" Dylan said. "You mean next week when the student companies sell our products?"

"No, dummy," Tom said, grinning. "The big party. I hear it's going to be a real blowout."

Dylan mumbled something, refusing to look at his brother. Even Tom had heard about the party!

"We'll have to get Kimberly a present," Tom said, taking careful aim at another tennis ball. "Got any ideas?"

"*You* got an invitation?" Dylan swung around to face his brother, his voice sharp.

Tom stopped mid-swing and looked back at his brother. "Didn't think I was one of the privileged ones, did you? She didn't invite many sixth graders, I understand."

Dylan couldn't answer. His throat seemed to close up, and the rush of anger made him dizzy.

His younger brother was invited, and Dylan had been left out!

"Anyway, it should be great." Tom went back to his tennis and didn't seem to notice how Dylan's face had contorted into a strange grimace.

Dylan mumbled something in answer and forced himself to move toward the house. He couldn't bring himself to confess the truth.

When Dylan entered the house, his mother was in the kitchen watching Tom practice as she stirred a bowl of brownie batter.

"How was school, dear?" she asked, sounding distracted. Then before Dylan even had time to answer she added, "Your brother's really showing promise as a tennis player, don't you think?"

"Of course," Dylan grunted. Why shouldn't his mother ignore him like everyone else?

He hurried to his room and shut the door behind him. Nobody cared about Dylan—not the kids at school, not even his own family. Tom was the one everyone liked, the son their parents took pride in. It was too much.

No one would even notice if I ran away, Dylan thought. *Yes, that's what I'll do. Run away.* But when he looked through his window at the gathering darkness outside, he shivered at the thought of being all alone.

It still sounded like a good idea, though. He'd just have to plan it out.

Saturday afternoon it was easy to slip away from the house. Tom had his tennis lesson, and Mrs. McKay had gone shopping. Dylan took his bike and rode down to the bus station.

He had made up his mind. He would buy a ticket to Los Angeles. In a big city, he could lie about his age and surely find a job. No one would be able to find him. Not that anyone was likely to bother looking, Dylan thought gloomily.

But inside the busy station, Dylan's plan began to weaken.

"I want a ticket to Los Angeles, please," he told

the man behind the counter when his turn came.

"That'll be fourteen-fifty," the man said without looking up.

Dylan felt his face redden. He didn't have enough money! "Uh, I'll be back later," he muttered, then walked quickly away from the window.

Frustrated, Dylan paced up and down. What could he do? He decided he'd just have to wait until next Friday, when he received his allowance for another week.

That was the day of the big party, Dylan remembered. Perfect. While everyone else went to Kimberly's house after school, Dylan would slip away to the bus station, and no one would even notice he was gone.

His mind made up, he started to walk to the exit and found Jessica Wakefield standing directly in front of him.

Dylan felt as if he'd been struck by lightning. All he could do was stare at the girl.

"Hi, Dylan," Jessica said. "What are you doing here?"

"Uh-h I-I—" he stammered. His confusion seemed to attract her attention. Jessica looked at him closely.

"Are you taking a trip?" she asked.

"Uh, yes." Dylan tried to think. "I'm going to see my aunt in San Francisco. Next week, I mean."

Jessica's interest was already waning, but Dylan

was too flustered to notice. "That's nice," she said absently, picking out an assortment of bus schedules. "Have you ever been there before?"

"Where?" Dylan blurted.

This time Jessica looked at him and frowned. "San Francisco," she reminded him.

"Uh, no. I mean yes, but not lately."

Jessica, deciding any attempt at conversation with this boy was useless, stuffed the schedules she had collected into her bag and turned to go. "See you," she said and hurried out the door, forgetting about Dylan and his confusion almost at once.

But Dylan, who didn't know Jessica very well, couldn't know that all thoughts of him were far from her mind the minute she left the station. He trembled with nervousness. Would Jessica tell? Did she suspect anything?

Maybe he should give up his plan to run away. No, Dylan reminded himself. He was still unwanted. He'd take his chances with Jessica. But now he had to get home before anyone else saw him. Dylan headed for the bike rack outside the station, unlocked his bike, climbed on, and pedaled furiously toward home.

Twelve

◇

On Monday Dylan didn't show up for the after-school meeting of his student company. On Tuesday Elizabeth found him sitting in a corner of the school library.

"Hi, Dylan," she said. "We missed you yesterday. We really need everyone in the group to help put the book together. Come on."

Dylan rejoined the rest of the students, ignoring their curious glances. He didn't speak to anyone, but he did his share of the work assembling the journals. The Sweet Valley Publishing Company, under Elizabeth's leadership, collated the group of student writings, duplicated it, bound it between bright cardboard covers, and stapled it together.

"It won't be much longer," Dylan told himself

under his breath, as he stapled pages together. "Friday is *the* day."

That thought helped him get through the next few days. Everyone else at school seemed to be having a great time. From Wednesday to Friday the sixth and seventh graders had an extended lunch period, so all the student companies could set up their booths and sell their products.

The *Sweet Valley Journal* made quite a hit; and Dylan, watching the other students crowd around their booth on Wednesday, almost felt a stirring of pride, thinking that he'd had a small part in creating the book.

"Looks great," Tom told his brother at lunch, holding up one of the books. "The only thing wrong with this book is that it doesn't have any of your work. Why didn't you submit something? Elizabeth told me she'd wanted to include you, after she found out what a good writer you were, but you didn't give her anything to consider."

Dylan looked up from his vegetable soup, surprised at the comment. How would Elizabeth Wakefield know—oh yes, she'd seen the essay he'd written. And thrown it away. She was probably just being polite.

Dylan mumbled an answer into his bowl.

"I'm going to look at the other booths—Group D has a Sweet Valley Trivia game to sell, and I've still got five dollars to spend. Then it's my turn to play salesman in our boutique," Tom said. "Want to come check out our stuff?"

"No, thanks." Dylan shook his head. The fog of misery that had engulfed him all week made it impossible to enjoy looking over the other companies' products, whether it was the cookies one company had baked or the stadium pillows another company was selling.

Finally Friday arrived, and Dylan spent the day watching the clock, waiting for school to be over so he could slip away to the bus station. He had enough money now for the ticket, but some of his enthusiasm for his plan seemed to have faded. The thought of being all alone, far away from his family, made Dylan feel strange inside, as if a million butterflies had invaded his stomach.

But if Dylan needed a reason to cling stubbornly to his earlier decision, all he had to do was listen. In every class, whenever the teacher wasn't looking, excited whispering ran around the room as the rest of the seventh graders discussed Kimberly's party.

"I bought her the new Johnny Buck album," Betsy Gordon said.

"I got her the cutest stuffed penguin," another seventh grader whispered back. "I can't wait for the party!"

When it was time for lunch, Dylan walked slowly down the hall, dreading the unfriendly faces in the cafeteria. As he hesitated outside the wide doors, he heard a group of eighth-grade students talking among themselves.

"Isn't that great?" one girl said. "A student from Sweet Valley winning the big state essay contest!"

"It sure is," another girl agreed. "That McKay boy—"

Dylan turned away sharply, not wanting to hear the rest. It wasn't enough that Tom was an outstanding athlete and immensely popular. Now Tom had won the big statewide essay contest, as well.

How unfair could life be?

Well, this news would give the whole school something to talk about, and Dylan's parents would be so excited they probably wouldn't notice that Dylan was unaccounted for that night.

"It's a perfect plan," Dylan said to himself. So why did he feel so miserable?

Dylan decided to skip lunch. He didn't want to hear any more talk about Kimberly's party or about Tom winning the contest. He headed back toward the school library, intending to lose himself in one of the study carrels until after lunch.

Meanwhile, Elizabeth thanked the remaining members of her company who had finished putting away the booth and adding the final touches to their reports and sales sheets. The last of their books had been sold, and Elizabeth felt a glow of pride as she realized how successful their project had been.

"I bet we get the highest grade of all," Amy said, dusting her hands as they finished collapsing the cardboard booth. "Mr. Bowman looked awfully pleased with us, Elizabeth."

"I don't know." Elizabeth shook her head. "The other groups have worked hard, too."

"But none of the other groups had a product as exciting as our *Sweet Valley Journal*," Amy boasted. "My mother was so thrilled with the one I brought home."

"Mine, too," Elizabeth said, smiling as she remembered her parents' pride. "Mom and Dad said we'd done a great job."

"We've got the rest of the extended lunch hour free," Amy said. "Want to go outside for a few minutes before we eat lunch?"

"No," Elizabeth answered. "I've been so busy at our booth I haven't had a chance to see the other companies' work. I'm going around to inspect the rest of the booths."

Amy decided to go along with Elizabeth to check out the Sweet Valley Vogue booth.

To their surprise, they found it almost deserted. Behind it, Jessica sat on a stool looking very bored.

"You don't have much left to sell," Amy noted, looking over the sparse collection of clothing and costume jewelry displayed at the front of the booth.

"That's great, Jess," Elizabeth said warmly. "You must have done really well."

"Well . . ." Jessica fiddled with a button on her blouse, glancing down at her almost empty cash box. "Not exactly."

"What do you mean, 'not exactly'?" Elizabeth's smile faded. She suddenly noticed a large bag of clothing partially hidden behind the booth. "What's all this?"

"You see," Jessica hurried to explain. "I liked Tamara's blouse, and she wanted my old pink scarf, so we traded. And Lila traded her white sweater for Kimberly's earrings, and . . ."

Elizabeth didn't know whether to laugh or cry. "Jess, if you and your group take all the best stuff out for yourselves, that leaves you with with nothing to sell. If you don't have any inventory, you can't make any money, and then you won't make a profit."

Jessica's expression darkened. She frowned at her sister for a long moment, then seemed to make up her mind about something. "Wait!" she called to two sixth graders who were about to walk past the booth. "Come and see our merchandise."

Pulling out the bag of reserved clothing, Jessica hastily hung the most enticing items around the front of the booth. "There." She nodded, as the two girls came closer, followed by more potential customers. "Will you be the salesperson for a few minutes, Lizzie?"

"Sure," Elizabeth agreed. "What are you going to do?"

Jessica looked determined. "I'm going to find the rest of my company." She sounded grim. "I've got to demote a bunch of vice presidents!"

Elizabeth and Amy giggled as Jessica hurried off. The new merchandise attracted so many buyers that Elizabeth remained busy handling the sales until Jessica returned. When only a couple of items were left, Elizabeth suggested they put them on sale. Jessica drew a line through the prices, marking down the remaining items. With that encouragement, the last of the boutique's inventory sold quickly. Then Jessica counted the profits and finished her financial statement.

Elizabeth hurried off to the cafeteria. Amy and Julie had been saving a seat for her, and Elizabeth put down her tray with a sigh.

"What a morning," she said. "I'm starved." She picked up the sloppy joe from her plate, trying not to drip tomato sauce.

"Have you heard the news?" Julie told them. "Ms. Pauley, our homeroom teacher, is leaving. That means we'll have a new teacher at school!"

Amy looked up from her sandwich in excitement. "I heard something better than that. Sweet Valley has a winner in the big state essay contest!"

"What?" Elizabeth almost choked on her sandwich. After she swallowed, she was able to say more clearly, "Who is it?"

"Dylan McKay. Can you believe it?" Amy looked astonished. "I felt sure you would win, Elizabeth. Or maybe *Tom* McKay. Everyone said his essay was good."

"That's because you didn't read Dylan's," Elizabeth explained. She felt a slight pang of regret; it would have been nice to win the contest herself. But she had a strong feeling that this recognition would be more important to Dylan McKay than it would have been to her.

Then she remembered. "Oh, no," she blurted out.

"What's wrong?" Amy asked, watching her friend. "I'm sorry you didn't win, Elizabeth."

"It's not that," Elizabeth explained quickly. "I haven't told Dylan that I entered his essay in the contest!"

"What are you talking about?" Julie said. The other two girls stared at Elizabeth in surprise. "Why would *you* enter Dylan's essay for him?"

"I'll explain it to you later," Elizabeth said. "Let's look for Dylan now. I just hope he isn't too angry."

"Why would he be mad? He won!" Julie looked even more confused.

"I know," Elizabeth said. "But Dylan's pretty hard to understand, sometimes. Come on, we've got to find him!"

Thirteen

Elizabeth forgot about her lunch as she jumped up from the table. The three girls walked around the lunchroom searching for Dylan while she explained how she had come to submit his essay for the competition. The bell rang before they could locate him; and Elizabeth, forced to give up, ran to her locker and collected her books for her next class.

When she got to her classroom she found she couldn't concentrate on the teacher's words. Instead Elizabeth stared at her book and heard an echo of Dylan's voice in her head. "Throw it away," he had said.

Didn't Dylan know that his writing revealed real talent?

Poor Dylan, Elizabeth thought. She had a feeling he didn't like being alone all the time. He was probably just too shy to try to make friends. And having a brother like Tom, who did so many things well, probably made it even worse.

Wincing, Elizabeth remembered the incident in the gym, when the kids in her group had been so obviously disappointed that Dylan was put in their group instead of Tom. She shook her head, even more determined to find Dylan and tell him about the essay. It was about time Dylan had a victory of his own to celebrate!

At the end of the period, Elizabeth bolted for the door and headed for the seventh-grade classrooms. She caught a glimpse of Dylan McKay entering the science classroom and quickened her pace. Thank goodness! Just as she was about to call his name, happy that her chase was over, she felt a tap on her shoulder.

"Just what I needed, another pair of arms!"

Elizabeth, startled, looked up to see Mrs. Arnette, her arms full of folders, peering down at her.

"Here," the teacher said. "You can help me carry these to class."

Elizabeth sighed, but it was impossible to refuse gracefully. She accepted a stack of folders and followed the teacher back down the hall.

She would just have to wait until after school to talk to Dylan. Another hour or two couldn't make that much difference, could it?

But when three o'clock finally came, and Elizabeth was released from her duties she found no trace of Dylan McKay.

"Good grief," Elizabeth murmured to herself. "How did he get out of the building so quickly?"

Had he left for the party already? Elizabeth looked up and saw Jessica conferring with several seventh-grade Unicorns at the end of the hall, and she walked over to join them.

"Hi, Lizzie," Jessica greeted her gaily. "Guess what! Ms. Wyler gave us an A on our project!"

"Actually, an A—," Tamara Chase corrected, but Jessica shrugged off this technicality.

"It's still an A," she pointed out.

"That's wonderful, Jess," Elizabeth said, her delight genuine. "I'm so glad. Mom and Dad will be so proud of you!"

"They should be," Jessica agreed. "But we deserved it. Don't you think?"

The twins exchanged a quick hug.

"I'm looking for Dylan McKay," Elizabeth told the girls. "I have something really important to tell him. Do you think he left for your party already, Kimberly?"

The dark-haired girl didn't seem to want to meet Elizabeth's inquiring gaze. Instead she stared down at the floor. "I don't think so," she muttered. "As a matter of fact, I didn't invite him, Elizabeth."

"What?" Elizabeth stared at the older girl. "I

thought everyone in the seventh grade was invited."

"Well, my parents told me to invite the whole class," Kimberly admitted. "But I just thought, well, Dylan's such a loner. He never wants to talk to anybody. . . ."

"I think he's just shy," Elizabeth interrupted, her voice stern. "What did you do, Kimberly?"

"I sort of *forgot* to give him his invitation," the other girl said, opening her notebook to reveal the one remaining invitation.

"That's terrible!" Elizabeth cried. "How do you think he must be feeling, knowing that everyone else is going?"

Kimberly turned red, and the other girls looked sheepish. But Jessica leaped to her fellow Unicorn's defense. "He probably doesn't even care," she told her sister. "What's the big deal?"

"I'll tell you what the big deal is," Elizabeth answered quickly. "Tom has lots of friends and does well in everything. Dylan's not as outgoing. Don't you think that must be hard for him, always being compared with his brother?"

"No," Jessica answered bluntly. "Why should it?"

"Jessica, think!" Elizabeth declared. "Remember how left out you felt when Mom and Dad were so excited about Steven's sports banquet last Friday? And at the banquet, when the coach said all those great things about his playing, you said Steven would have a terribly swelled head."

"Well, he did," Jessica tossed her long blond hair over her shoulder and shrugged. "All he's talked about this week is his new letter and how next year he's going to win the Most Valuable Player award. And Mom and Dad were just as bad. 'Steven this' and 'Steven that'! It was disgusting."

"If you felt that way, how do you think Dylan feels?" Elizabeth asked her twin.

Jessica's angry grimace faded. "I never thought of that," she said.

The other girls looked ashamed as well. "I guess I should have invited Dylan," Kimberly admitted. "What can I do now, Elizabeth?"

"We'll have to find him and tell him that you forgot to give him his invitation," Elizabeth decided. "It's not exactly true, but it will have to do."

Kimberly and Tamara agreed to check out the gym, and the Wakefield twins ran outside to search the school grounds.

But Dylan couldn't be found anywhere.

"I don't understand it," Elizabeth said, looking worried. "Where could he have gone?"

Jessica, despite her charitable impulse, was getting impatient. "Who knows?" She shrugged. "That boy turns up in the strangest places. Last week I saw him in the bus station."

"The bus station?" Elizabeth stared at her twin. "What was he doing there?"

"I don't know, Lizzie. Oh, yeah." Jessica suddenly remembered. "He said something about visiting an aunt in San Francisco."

"In the middle of the school year?" Elizabeth frowned. "That doesn't make sense, Jess."

"Who said Dylan McKay ever made sense?" Jessica retorted. "I've got to go, Elizabeth. I told Kimberly I'd help her get the party started. I can't be late. Are you coming?"

"Not yet," Elizabeth said. "You go ahead. I've got to find Dylan."

"Here comes Kimberly," Jessica said, as she exited the school building with Tamara and Tom McKay. "Did you find him?"

Kimberly shook her head. "Even Tom doesn't know where he is," she said.

Tom McKay was frowning. "Hi." He nodded at the twins. "I didn't know that Dylan hadn't gotten his invitation. I feel really dumb. No wonder he's been so quiet all week."

"I've got to go," Kimberly interrupted, "or the guests will be there before I am! If you find Dylan, will you give his this?" She thrust the envelope bearing Dylan's name toward Elizabeth.

"You go ahead," Elizabeth said, taking the invitation. "I'm going to keep looking."

"Me, too," Tom added, as the other girls walked away. "I called home, but Mom said that Dylan isn't there."

"Oh no," Elizabeth said. "Tom, Jessica said that

she saw Dylan at the bus station last week, and he mentioned going to visit your aunt in San Francisco."

"What?" Tom looked confused. "We don't have an aunt in San Francisco!"

Elizabeth was more disturbed than ever. "I think we'd better get to the bus station," she urged.

They both began to run.

Fourteen

◇

Elizabeth and Tom covered the blocks to the bus station in record time. When they reached the small brick building, Elizabeth raced through the front doors.

Several of the afternoon buses were about to leave. Elizabeth pushed through a group of college students carrying knapsacks, pausing to scan the faces of two boys at the end of the building, but they were strangers.

Tom, panting, caught up with her. "Do you see him?"

"No." Elizabeth shook her head. She felt a strange sense of urgency. "I hope we're not too late!"

"There are more people out back boarding the afternoon bus to L.A.," Tom said.

"Let's go," Elizabeth said, and they hurried to the back entrance.

The line of people waiting to board the bus included a woman carrying a baby, two sailors in uniform, an old man with a beard, and—Dylan!

The bus driver was collecting tickets as the passengers moved forward. Dylan had almost reached the front of the line when Elizabeth grabbed his arm.

"Dylan, wait!"

The tall boy spun around, astonished.

"Elizabeth?" he sputtered. "Tom? What are you doing here?"

"What are *you* doing here? That's the question," Tom said to his brother. He sounded angry. "I've been worried about you! What do you think you're doing, anyhow?"

A woman behind Dylan stared at them curiously, while behind her a man called out, "Who's holding up the line?"

Reluctantly, Dylan stepped out of the line.

Elizabeth drew a deep breath, trying to make her heart stop pounding.

"Dylan, where were you going?" she asked.

Unable to fabricate an imaginary relative under his brother's indignant gaze, Dylan hesitated. "I was running away," he muttered.

Tom gaped at him. "Of all the stupid things to do," Tom blustered. "I'd like to knock your block off!" But he looked more anxious than angry, and Dylan stared at him as if in surprise.

"I thought you'd all be at the party by now. I didn't think you'd notice I was gone," he said.

"The party? Is that why you pulled this stupid stunt?" Tom demanded. "Do you think I could have a good time at somebody's silly birthday party if my own brother was missing?"

Dylan stared into his brother's face. "Would you really care?"

"Of course I would, you dummy!" Tom said affectionately. "You're my brother. Do you think you can just walk out of the family?"

Dylan seemed speechless. "I didn't think you'd mind if I left," he murmured at last. He seemed to relax a little. "I didn't think anyone wanted me around, that's all. Mom and Dad always seem to be talking about what *you've* done, and all the kids at school like you, not me. I just felt left out."

"Here." Elizabeth pulled out the envelope with Dylan's name on it. "Kimberly forgot to give you your invitation, Dylan. She told me to tell you she's very sorry, and hopes you'll come to the party anyhow."

Dylan stared at the envelope but didn't make a move to accept it. "That's not true. She didn't forget," he said. "She just didn't want me to come."

Elizabeth sighed. "You're right. She didn't forget. But she *is* sorry. Honestly, Dylan. And we all really want you to come."

The sincerity in her voice seemed to reach him, because Dylan's frown faded. "Why? Tom's the one everyone likes."

"Tom's easy to like," Elizabeth admitted. "He's so friendly, and he's always joking around."

"I'm not like Tom," Dylan muttered, looking down at the pavement.

"So what?" Tom demanded. "You don't have to be like me for people to like you."

"Dylan, don't you think that some of the kids at school like Jessica better than they do me?" Elizabeth asked.

Dylan seemed startled. He lifted his gaze from the ground to look into her eyes. "You really think so?"

Elizabeth smiled, thinking of Lila and the other Unicorns. "Jessica's fun to be around, too; she likes to talk and joke and party. Some of her friends think I'm too serious. But, Dylan, just because I like different things doesn't mean that I'm not a likeable person, too. I have my own friends."

Dylan stared at her.

"Maybe you need to try a little harder, yourself," Elizabeth said. "How will people know how nice you are if you don't give them the opportunity to find out? You don't have to do what Tom does; find out what you do well."

They both stared at Dylan, and he flushed. "But it's easy for Tom," he protested. "He's good at lots of things; I'm just a loser."

"That's not true!" Tom said.

"Tom's right," Elizabeth added. "What about the contest?"

Dylan looked perplexed. "I heard that Tom won the state contest," he said.

"No, I didn't, Dylan," Tom crowed. "*You* won the contest."

"That's impossible," Dylan protested. "I didn't even mail in my essay."

Elizabeth turned red. She shifted from one foot to the other and looked at the ground. "I mailed in your essay," she confessed. "It was just too good to throw away. I knew you told me to, Dylan, but I couldn't. Please don't be angry."

"I can't believe it," Dylan murmured. "Everyone said you wrote such a good essay, Tom."

"Well, mine might have been okay, but yours was better," Tom said. "You won. And I'm really proud of you, Dylan."

Elizabeth held her breath while the two boys looked at each other, their faces solemn. Then, almost at the same instant, they both grinned broadly.

Tom pounded his brother on the back. "That's my big brother!" he shouted.

"Now, what about that party?" Elizabeth demanded. "Are you going to show the seventh grade the new Dylan McKay?"

"Let's go," Dylan agreed bravely, with a new confidence he would never have guessed he could feel. But with a brother like Tom, and a friend like

Elizabeth Wakefield—he grinned a bit shyly at the pretty blond-haired girl—how could he be afraid? "Look out, Sweet Valley, here we come!"

Dylan and Tom McKay showed up at the Haver residence only half an hour late for the party. Elizabeth, who had just arrived herself, after having gone home to drop off her books, saw Kimberly hurry to welcome the two latecomers.

"Hi, Kimberly," Tom said. He handed the birthday girl a neatly wrapped package. "This is from both of us," he told her, winking at Dylan.

Kimberly accepted the package, smiling first at Tom, then Dylan. "Thanks, guys," she said. "Dylan, I'm sorry about the late invitation. I'm really glad you came."

Dylan seemed startled by her apparent sincerity, then he grinned at her.

"I think it's so exciting about your winning the state contest," Kimberly went on. "You're going to be in all the newspapers, I bet! Come in and tell us about it."

Taking Dylan's arm, she pulled him into the center of the party.

Tom, left alone, grinned at Elizabeth.

"Guess it's my turn to be the Lone Ranger," he quipped.

Elizabeth laughed. There was no danger of Tom's being ignored. But it was nice to see everyone crowding around Dylan, congratulating him and demanding details about the winning essay. Elizabeth noted the shy smile that lit up Dylan's long face and thought how much better he looked when he smiled.

"Lizzie!" Jessica suddenly appeared at Elizabeth's side. "Where have you been? What's going on here? What's everyone talking to Dylan about?"

"He won the state essay contest," Elizabeth reminded her.

"Oh, right," Jessica said, not really interested. "That's nice."

Elizabeth laughed. "Yes. I think it's terrific," she said.

Suddenly Jessica remembered the exciting news she had to tell Elizabeth. "Did you hear that Ms. Pauley is leaving?" she asked her twin. "Caroline Pearce says she heard that the new teacher is a man! I hope he's good-looking."

"Oh, Jess. What difference does it make?" Elizabeth had to laugh at her sister. She certainly didn't care if it was a man or a woman. "I'm sure our new teacher will be nice, no matter what."

What will the new teacher be like? Find out in Sweet Valley Twins #17, **BOYS AGAINST GIRLS.**

SWEET VALLEY TWINS

Tell your kid sister, your sister's friends and your friends' sisters . . . Now they can all read about Jessica and Elizabeth in SWEET VALLEY TWINS—a brand-new series written just for them.

You love reading about the Wakefield twins, and the whole gang at SWEET VALLEY HIGH. Now there's something new and exciting—it's Francine Pascal's latest series—SWEET VALLEY TWINS. These are the stories about Jessica and Elizabeth when they are just twelve years old, as all the Sweet Valley excitement begins.

☐	26741	DOUBLE LOVE #1	$2.75
☐	26621	SECRETS #2	$2.75
☐	26627	PLAYING WITH FIRE #3	$2.75
☐	26746	POWER PLAY #4	$2.75
☐	26742	ALL NIGHT LONG #5	$2.75
☐	26813	DANGEROUS LOVE #6	$2.75
☐	26622	DEAR SISTER #7	$2.75
☐	26744	HEARTBREAKER #8	$2.75
☐	26626	RACING HEARTS #9	$2.75
☐	26620	WRONG KIND OF GIRL #10	$2.75
☐	26824	TOO GOOD TO BE TRUE #11	$2.75
☐	26688	WHEN LOVE DIES #12	$2.75
☐	26619	KIDNAPPED #13	$2.75
☐	26764	DECEPTIONS #14	$2.75
☐	26765	PROMISES #15	$2.75
☐	26740	RAGS TO RICHES #16	$2.75
☐	26883	LOVE LETTERS #17	$2.75
☐	26687	HEAD OVER HEELS #18	$2.75
☐	26823	SHOWDOWN #19	$2.75
☐	26959	CRASH LANDING! #20	$2.75

Prices and availability subject to change without notice.

Buy them at your local bookstore or use this convenient coupon for ordering: